THE GLASS BOAT

ALISON WARD

Brilliance Books

First Edition Brilliance Books 1983
Copyright © Alison Ward 1983
Brilliance Books 14 Clerkenwell Green London EC1
England

Brilliance Books thanks the Labour controlled Greater
London Council and all our friends for financial support.

ISBN Hardback 0 946189 40 4
ISBN Paperback 0 946189 45 5

Typeset by MC Typeset of Chatham Kent. Printed and
bound by Nene Litho & Woolnough Bookbinding, both
of Wellingborough Northants

In a man's world, women have to struggle much harder to wake up.

Not so Asmodus.

Asmodus awoke at the dawning of noon. He was the first to get up, and despised Pink for sleeping on and missing the best part of the day. By then the sun – when it shone – would have drawn up the mist from the Thames, and the swans would float by, looking up, waiting to be fed. Asmodus padded to the window and threw some bread down into the water, wondering if swans flew away in the winter. At least when winter came there would be no more tourist-boats, loud-speakers blaring their distorted patter all over the river. Asmodus knew their script by heart, and mouthed along with it while he scrutinised himself in the mirror and snipped at his hair.

"To your left, ladies and gentlemen, these derelict wharves bear witness to the fabulous wealth of past centuries. Tall ships once tied up at Gabriel's Wharf; their cargoes were tea and spices, silver and slaves. It is said that the infamous Ned Quint kept his den of thieves by the creek side . . . as we pass by the once-throbbing heart of the city's dockland, we may feel a pang of regret for its past glories . . .".

Asmodus leaned out of the window and waved at the backside of the boat. "Lies, rubbish!" he called. "Don't listen to it." But sometimes there were strange noises at the wharf, loose chains grating against the stonework and a smell of cloves that drifted in through the cracks. The place was supposed to be haunted but he didn't care. It was a home for him and Pink, and as a home it was vastly preferable to the Old Embassy Squat or the rainbow-coloured condemned houses behind the railway station.

He wandered from room to room, exulting in the space and air and dusty sunlight, and finally climbed out onto the roof. On one side, the grandest river-view in London, the whole steaming, glittering Thames rushing past. The other side looked down into a central courtyard, cracked paving-stones, dank, stained with oil and rubbish; Pink's old van rusting away in a corner. It looked a mess. Asmodus, peeping over the parapet, would often ponder about what could be done to improve it. Today . . . .

Today there was something else down there. A black car, and two people peering up at the walls and pointing, a grey man and a young woman whose hair was so fair it looked almost white in the courtyard gloom. The man leaned back against the car and swept out his hand generously, as though he owned the whole wharf and was giving it to the woman. Then he folded his arms and seemed to crack a joke, because the woman stopped looking thoughtful and smiled – a lazy, wide smile whose sweetness astonished Asmodus and affected the man deeply. He drew the woman to him, began kissing her, and the tiredness went out of his face. Asmodus couldn't see the woman's expression because her back was turned, but there was a tension in her shoulders; perhaps she sensed that she was being watched.

Asmodus shrank down behind the parapet, feeling vaguely resentful. He ought to appear in full view, high above them, an imperious silhouette before the sun, and call out: "Would you leave now? And shut the gate behind you." But then, they might ask him to do the same thing. It all depended on what they were doing here. He leaned his head back against the warm stones and tried to dream identities for them.

Perhaps they were from the Council, come to wring their hands over wharves, eyesores and health-hazards, wondering whether to solve the problem by setting up a committee, or whether to refer it to some higher authority at the Ministry of Government. People from Councils didn't matter, any more than people from Preservation Societies. Was there a Preservation Society for Old Wharves? Asmodus thought of fund-raising coffee-mornings, to restore the curlicues around the loading-bay.

No, the strangers didn't look like people who restored curlicues.

Asmodus sighed. He supposed that the wharf had an owner, somewhere. The man looked as though he owned all sorts of things. Maybe he'd bought the wharf as a birthday present for the woman. Oh darling, what a sweet little wharf! Just what I've always wanted.

Asmodus gave up. He would deal with them when the time came. They might not come back for weeks, or months. Or ever. He put his eye to a chink in the stonework and concentrated his evil stare on them, willing them to go away.

*

"They use special machines, to smash walls this thick." The man took his hands out of his pockets and caressed the stonework, as though he'd built the walls himself.

The woman didn't answer. She stood a little way off, feeling trapped.

"You're not upset, are you?" The man's voice was anxious. "Aren't you pleased? Haven't you always wanted to tackle something this big? Stéphane, I'm talking to you."

She excused herself. "Us architects have an instinct for old buildings, didn't you know? This one gives me the feeling it doesn't want us."

Why do I always forget, he thought, that she needn't see things the same way that I see them? He took Stéphane's hands and smiled at her. "That's the difference between us. You think about the wharf as it is, and all I think about is what it's going to be. I'm sorry. I didn't mean to rush you with all my ideas. You need time to get used to them. Let's talk about something else. I haven't even told you how I came to buy it."

Gabriel's Wharf had come his way as part of a much larger deal over an industrialised site further east. He, Martin, had been amazed that the previous owners had no idea what to do with the wharf: they'd let it stand empty for twenty years and they even seemed glad to get rid of it. It was incredible that people could be so stupid. The site was the important thing, not the building at all; to him, the possibilities of the site were so obvious that he'd bought it without even bothering to argue about the price. Now he saw it for himself, he knew he was right.

Stéphane let him talk on, his vision rising out of the river, a great

3

complex of flats to be built on the site of Gabriel's Wharf. He hardly mentioned the millions it was going to cost. He was trying to share the vision itself, and his way of doing it was to have her draw up the plans.

She wondered whether her senior partner knew about that.

"Harkness agrees," Martin said. "I talked to him about it last week. He said something about giving it to young Adam, but I insisted on you. I said, Adam's done some good designs for me, factories and things like that, but he hasn't got Stéphane's taste."

"You told Mr Harkness that?"

"Why not? He knows you're not going to be one of his hacks for ever. Show him! You can do this one. You could do it in your sleep."

"Maybe," she said drily, "that's what worries me. I do too many things in my sleep."

"What are you talking about? How strange you are." He caught her up in a suffocating hug. She wasn't like other women: she never asked him for anything, didn't run around with younger men, respected the way he felt about his wife, never sulked when he went away; tantalising to be with, delicious to sleep with.

She kept so much of herself hidden.

"I promise," he whispered, "to keep you awake all night. If you promise to build this one with me. Say yes. Yes?"

"Yes, sir." She put her hand on his chest and pushed him back, gently, towards the car. "I'll start on it right away."

"Just like that?"

"Just like that. Tomorrow, if you like."

"No, you won't. Tomorrow's Sunday, remember? I'm going to take you away somewhere nice."

"Where?"

"Wait and see."

On Sundays, the wharf could be miserable. When Asmodus and Pink had some money, they generally went out on Sundays; otherwise, they resigned themselves to passing the time as drearily as possible. Asmodus stared, morose, at the television set. He had turned the sound off, but the images were still fatuous; like the commentary. Mr and Mrs Bald Eagle and Baby Bald Eagle. At

4

home. Cut to a scruffy solitary bald eagle hunched on the edge of a dripping tree. Obviously not taking any pride in its personal appearance. Probably unloved unmarried bald eagle. With no object in life. Not like Mr and Mrs Bald Eagle, so purposefully finding insects to stuff down Baby Bald Eagle's throat. Now you eat up all those spiders' legs, or you can't have this nice greenfly. Think of all the starving little bald eagles in China . . .

Asmodus sniffed the air appreciatively.

"Little Pink, what are you smoking?"

"Nothing. Just some stuff Nancy gave me. Ages ago. It's not very good."

"Really? You seem to be well away on it."

"Don't buzz me, Asmodus, I got to concentrate and fill in this Social Security thing."

The first question was simple enough. It required you to tick either a box marked "male" or a box marked "female". Absently, Pink ticked both boxes and moved on. The questions seemed to be arranged in order of difficulty: for the next one you had to delete whichever was inapplicable of married/single/divorced/widowed/separated. Pink couldn't decide what to delete, so he didn't delete anything. Next one. Date of birth: 39th Februber 1066. Previous jobs: nightwatchman, scullery-maid. Easy, once you got into the swing of it. Hobbies.

Hobbies?

"Asmodus?"

Pause. "Speak."

"What do they want to know your hobbies for?"

"Hobbies, hobbies. Ah yes, it's a 'measure of stability', I believe they call it. If you're pottering about at home with ships in bottles they know you can't be out all the time drinking, dancing, and having one-night stands."

"Oh." Pink made a sincere effort to think of something, anything he did which might be classed as a hobby. Watching Television, he wrote, then crossed it out in desperation and substituted, Going to the Toilet.

"Oh, I don't want to do this anymore. It's too hard."

"Don't do it then. I've told you before, you don't have to do anything just because Mr Sharpe says so. The way he goes on, anyone would think he ran the Social Security all by himself single-handed. He doesn't know anything."

"I hate Mr Sharpe. D'you know, last time he told me there were thousands of jobs I could do."

Asmodus treated this folly with the scorn it deserved. In his opinion there were only five jobs: office, dish-washer, the armed forces, factory, and shop-assistant. Some people just didn't fit into any of the five jobs. Mr Sharpe was so out of touch he didn't realise that it was actually cheaper to keep artists like Pink on social security, rather than worrying about finding unsuitable jobs for them to do. Mr Sharpe had even suggested once that he, Asmodus, should get a job in a factory making truck axles. Truck axles! And when the factory laughed at the very idea of employing Asmodus, Mr Sharpe sent him to a special centre. It was supposed to re-habilitate the chronic unemployed, make them get up early and do something from nine to five. Asmodus had managed to spend nine to five drinking tea and reading the newspaper. None of Mr Sharpe's ideas worked. It was obvious why they didn't work. They were totally inappropriate. But Asmodus had proved that if you stuck to your guns long enough, Mr Sharpe ran out of ideas and left you alone.

Asmodus allowed his indignation to wear itself out in a sigh, and he settled down with Pink to stare out of the window. For a while they sat quite still, watching rain sweep in gusts across the river, until lights began to appear on the opposite shore: their reflections like broken stars shining up through the dull water. Asmodus half-closed his eyes and felt the twilight drifting through the lower floors, rising up to the place where he sat. Somewhere far away, a door banged.

He jerked his head round and listened.

"Did you hear that?"

Pink groaned and settled his head more comfortably on a cushion. "It's only the wind moving things. It always does that, Asmodus, why are you so twitchy today?"

"I thought someone was downstairs, that's all. Don't sit there yawning. Go and look. No. On second thoughts, I'll go myself."

"Anyone would think you're expecting someone." Pink sat up. "Are you? Who d'you think's going to bother coming here?

Nobody ever comes to see us these days."

Asmodus chewed at his thumbnail and wondered whether he ought to tell Pink about yesterday's strangers.

"And besides," Pink babbled on triumphantly, "if anyone was there, we'd soon know because the cats would get them. Listen. The cats've all come up."

Asmodus sank back into his cushions. The cats had indeed come up. He recognised the furtive slithering and squeaking outside the door. They seemed to come up earlier every evening.

"Oh well." He stood up and stretched. "Time to throw them another tin of that disgusting dog food, I suppose. No, wait."

The cats had got someone. There was a sinister flurry of scattering and mewling, which was cut off in a thin squawk.

"Get out my way, stupid, you want me to break my neck?"

Asmodus and Pink grinned at each other.

"Hi, Nancy, shut the door quick."

The wind from the stairs fluttered briefly among the Honourable Nancy Whitton's clothes.

"Can't you tie those cats up, or something? They always act like they haven't been fed in centuries."

"They haven't got much else to think about."

"Yeah. Poor things." Nancy folded both arms around Asmodus and Pink together, while they savoured the timeless Nancy-smell of teachests, with Indian hemp undertones.

"Nancy! Why don't you come to see us more often, my love? Coffee?"

"I told you, I was working on this Xanadu idea – yes please, black." Nancy circled the table, looking for something new, and fastened on a tin horse beside the bed. Pink explained how Asmodus had found the horse in the river, one day when the tide was out, and had made Pink drag it all the way up to their room, and wash it in the bath. Pink thought it was a roundabout horse, and he couldn't decide what colour to paint it. What colour did Nancy think? But Nancy had lost interest in the horse, and interrupted him:

"I haven't seen that photo before, have I?"

"Which photo, my love?" Asmodus smiled, knowing perfectly well which photo she meant. It was in a silver frame by his side of the bed, taking pride of place during the twelve days of his wedding anniversary. He looked round.

"Oh, that one, yes. It's a photo of Dasha."

"Who?"

"My wife, you know." Asmodus waved his hand vaguely, enjoying the puzzled expression on Nancy's face. He knew what she was thinking: Asmodus, famous Queen of the Night, married? Nancy's first impulse would be to shriek, "Are you crazy, or something?" But she wouldn't want to appear naive. She stared at the photograph, and a whip cracked in her imagination.

"Look at that face! What I could do with a face like that in my Xanadu piece."

"Yes, indeed. A face to launch a thousand videodramas."

Asmodus looked proudly over Nancy's shoulder. If he had loved women, he would have loved Dasha: arrogant Polish-American wandering spirit who was part of his soul, not certainly feminine, certainly not masculine. As it was, he had been content to marry her, years ago when she was a student in London, and thought she wanted to stay there for ever. She lived in Paris now, but every year they sent each other photographs on their wedding anniversary: Dasha never criticised his snapshots, which was kind of her because she made her living as a photographer. He had invited her to see his new home at the wharf. He expected her to arrive one day soon, maybe next week . . .

His voice trailed off. Nancy wasn't listening. She, passing through the curtain of Dasha's high cheekbones and narrow dark eyes, had gone into orbit over Xanadu, the courts of the Great Khans, and the barbaric splendour of the Golden Horde in the days when all Europe was young. Her next videodrama would dazzle a jaded public with these enchantments. It would be made at the wharf. Dasha must be in it.

Asmodus would need persuading that these were brilliant ideas. Nancy reached for her bag and hunted inside it, thoughtfully, for something to cloud his mind.

*

MgGrills.

St Pincer.

Frogs de Boulogne.

Stéphane grinned.

"I'm sorry, you'll have to type it again. Look – I'll print it out for you. *Maître Gilles, Société Poincert, Forges de Boulogne.* The agency said you were bilingual."

"Yes." The girl stared out of the window. Her eyes were vacant green and quite beautiful. Stéphane leaned back in her chair and felt tired. Madamina, she thought, I needn't waste my charm on you. You will be immune to it. She sat forward suddenly, and her chair made a little snapping sound.

"If you can't read my writing, ask me, all right? All right. Please bring it back as soon as you've finished. And shut the door."

Fine, don't shut the door then. Me shut the door. Softly. This office needs tidying up. Oh, I don't want to do that. Who says architects should be tidy? Only the cleaning woman.

The cleaning woman came to work in an old yellow Mercedes and left notes in Stéphane's ashtray saying "Please do not drop your ash all over the desk." Stéphane looked at her wastepaper basket overflowing with strips of paper. The cleaning woman would never know how much failed effort those strips of paper represented. One more day's work on the wharf project.

Stéphane swung gently in her chair, with her arms dangling, gazing into the distance.

On good days, her plans for the wharf project only seemed uninspired. On bad days, they looked almost brutal. The designs she did before had love in them somewhere. Only, nobody had praised those designs like they praised this: one gold star for its cost, another for its size, and nought out of ten for its soul. She tore up another strip of paper, carefully, into tiny flakes, imagining herself walled up inside the design as though it were already so many thousand tons of concrete and steel. We're not in the sixth form anymore, Stéphane; we don't make successes of ourselves by always getting ten out of ten, we do it by taking favours from the right people.

Stéphane frowned. There was a kind of sadness she felt when she saw the dawn after being awake all night: she had felt sad that way when Martin took her to see the wharf. He wanted to build something special out of it, to share with her. Perhaps. He never said so. Too used to acting the grand magnate, bestowing gifts on his favoured ones. She remembered him stretching out his arm in a generous sweep: "It's all yours. Go ahead and make a name for yourself with it. It's what you deserve." She deserved it? She deserved it all. That was when she felt sad, but he didn't understand her mood and cracked a silly joke, so that she smiled to show him it didn't matter.

Somebody knocked at the door.

"Come in."

"My dear, what's wrong?" Stéphane's visitor came to sit on the edge of her desk. "It can't be that bad. Tell Uncle Adam about it."

"Nothing. I was thinking about the wharf."

"Oh, that." He nodded carefully, and pulled at his moustache. "I keep telling you, don't take it so seriously. Nobody's going to care what you do with the wharf. Everyone will say it's wonderful, just so long as you keep Martin happy."

"Suppose I don't?"

He shuddered. "Failing to keep our biggest client happy? People have got the sack for less. And don't forget I introduced him to you. Look, don't be silly. Why shouldn't you keep him happy? Doesn't he make you happy?"

"No he doesn't." Stéphane gazed out of the window, and fidgeted. "Is it still only half-past three?"

Adam felt sorry for her: she was looking very pale these days. She spent too much time in the artificial light of conference rooms and, as he suspected, glittering basements where women charmed each other fleetingly in dark mirrors, playing some soft fragrant, wistful pretence at loving. He knew all that because he had read about it in paperbacks from airport bookstalls. He wondered if Martin knew what Stéphane got up to. Probably he did know, but so long as Martin thought he was in control of a thing, he never saw any harm in it. Poor old Martin. Stéphane didn't know what love was, and Adam had long ago given up trying to teach her.

"Never mind," he said, picking up a folder he had brought in with him. "Have a look at these. Three lovely young ladies, all dying to be our new secretary. Big international firm of City architects requires big international secretary. The bigger the better. How about this one?"

She took the hint. Snap out of it, the wharf's a bore, it's only a job, choosing a new secretary's more fun so let's concentrate on that. Stéphane's mind slipped into other people's points of view like a gear-shift that clicked easily some days, or today made a grating whine that set her teeth on edge. Much heartless laughter at Adam's jokes about interviewing the new girls, good morning, let's get straight to the point, sit on my knee and we'll talk about the first thing that pops up.

"Here," he said, pushing a photograph across the desk, "what d'you think of her?"

"Hmm." Ringlets and a dazzling smile.

Stéphane flipped it back at him. "I wouldn't like to meet her on a bright sunny day. Next?"

"This one's even better."

"I didn't know you liked Orientals."

"Lovely creatures, scented butterflies."

"Yes, but can she do the job?" Dear Agony Auntie, where can I get an O-level in prettiness? Signed, unemployed.

"Objection overruled. Give her back. Thank you." Adam closed the file. "Your famous sense of taste isn't working today, is it? Forget the girls then. Leave it all to me. Look, here's another file for a new teaboy. Charlie's going at the end of the month. Silly little fairy. He only wanted to save enough money to go to Amsterdam, so he's stopping work. Can you imagine that?"

"Good for him."

"Yes, well, I don't want to bother about his replacement either." Adam dangled the teaboy file to show it was empty. "I'll just give it to the Jobshop and let them poke around in their woodwork for something. Shall I?"

"If you like."

"Moan, drone. If I were you, I'd take the rest of the day off and get drunk."

She smiled, and said something about walking beside her own shoes. Sometimes she said things he didn't quite understand; obscure French things, he supposed, quite charming. She apologised for her mood by explaining that tomorrow was her thirtieth birthday.

"Is that so. Never mind, we all grow old. Give me your hand." He pulled her to her feet. "Now then. Dance with me, to celebrate."

One step forward, two back, and aside. Curious ritual patterns from a time when men were men, and women were women, and there wasn't anything else.

"Adam, will you lend me your boat?"

"Most certainly, my dear. What for?"

Hands up, hands down, twirl around:

"I want to look at the wharf from the river."

"That's boring. Try again."

Two and a-three, slow, slow:

"I shall sail by the stars, to an island at the end of the world."

"Where love lasts for ever and ever?"

"In all the seven seas, no such place exists." Stéphane laughed. "Let go my hand, someone'll come in and catch us."

"That's better. Seriously now, don't worry about everything so much. Just knock your wharf down, build Martin what he wants, and everyone will be happy. Take my word for it."

*

"Have one of these orange ones, Nancy, those greeny things aren't much good, are they?"

Asmodus handed his pill-tray round for second helpings, rare extravagance reserved for special occasions. Asmodus was so excited he had forgotten that the greeny things were a present from Nancy, but she forgave him and settled down to enjoy the effects of an orange one.

Pink had told her that Asmodus had spent the whole week, really the whole week, preparing for Dasha's visit: sewing up cushions and painting tables and worrying about what to wear and ringing up the airport to make sure the flight hadn't been cancelled. The airport had been very patient with him: no, there was no cancellation, no circumstance beyond their control, not even a tiny delay, the flight would arrive at its scheduled time tonight. Asmodus had made a timetable looking like a plan for military manoeuvres, but essentially all it meant was, four till seven, refreshments; seven till eight-thirty, get to the airport; nine o'clock, meet Dasha.

It was still only half past six, but Pink was giving his fingernails a final scrape and wondering whether his hair would dry in time. Nancy winked at him, because she was about to set Asmodus off again on the only possible topic of conversation.

"Did you ever meet her parents?"

Asmodus raised his eyebrows. He always avoided the subject of parents, out of politeness. In Nancy's case, because he had a vague idea that the parents of Honourables were usually divorced, and as for Dasha, that Polish parents who went to America had probably suffered a great deal, best left unspoken.

"No,"he said, "I never did. She didn't talk about them, not in the Great Art Gallery Squat days, anyway."

When they were married he had carried Dasha over the threshold of the Great Art Gallery Squat. They lived there for over six months, with their respective lovers who had been witnesses at the registry-office nuptials. "In fact," he went on, "she didn't say much about America at all."

"Yeah, but she must have told you why she didn't want to go back?"

"As far as I can remember, her exact words were, 'I can't stand to be in a roomful of Yanks. They ain't got no culture'."

"Doesn't sound like she had much herself."

"An absolute gangster," said Asmodus fondly. "The dear child. But that was years ago, you'd never know it now. In six months I transformed her into a perfect aristocrat. It wasn't easy."

He sighed, remembering the storms that blew up when he criticised Dasha's manners. If he went on too long, she even used to throw things at him. All sorts of things. Milk bottles, and vibrators, and cats. Rich, lively times in the Great Art Gallery Squat. Nothing since had been as much fun.

"You're getting sentimental, Asmodus."

"D'you think so? Well, get your things together, my loves. It's time to go. Does it look better if I leave these buttons undone? Or not?"

*

Dasha enjoyed flying. The aeroplane moving up to the runway, gliding through pathways of coloured lights, the wings extending themselves like claws, silently in the dark. It stood on the runway for a long time, massive shadow filled with light, suffocating and expectant. Then the sound of the engines changed and it moved forward, between the parallel golden strips that met in infinity;

Dash could never feel the exact moment the wheels left the ground, however hard she concentrated.

Climbing away from the city, she saw there was a mist covering its lights like a cobweb: spell-bound Paris, asleep for a hundred years. Be awake when I come back.

When there was nothing more to see except her own reflection, she settled back in her seat and thought about Asmodus. What did he want to go and live in a wharf for? He was still the strangest, most unpredictable . . . but he seemed content with it, that was important. And he would ask her all sorts of questions like money, and happy, and she didn't know if she would be able to answer them. Well, not money perhaps. Last time she saw him, he was writing a pamphlet castigating the illusory nature of money. Made a change from all that end-of-the-world stuff he used to churn out, or maybe it didn't. His pamphlets would never be best-sellers. Neither would the photographs that she wanted to take, thought were worth taking. She and Asmodus could always find a good grudge to pick over together.

They had so much in common, choosing presents for him was a pleasure. She reviewed her offerings: a bottle of cognac, one starry gold earring – the other one she wore in her own ear – and a new recording of Mozart's Requiem. Asmodus adored Requiems, he had at least six in his collection.

And so they would drink the brandy and listen to the music, Asmodus would announce that only Latin could express true grandeur of thought, then she would disagree with him. You understood Latin only inside your own head, where you lent it grandeur if you liked, or the sanctified sweetness of incense, or the enduring clarity of marble. According to fashion, you made your choice. Dasha smiled. Tiredness always made her imagined conversations perfectly satisfying. Fragments of the music ran around in her mind, repeating themselves like a tape loop. She was still hearing them when the plane landed; they moved in rhythm with her footsteps down the eternal plastic corridors to Passport Control.

Benedictus,
qui venit,
in nom . . . .

"How long do you intend staying here, Mrs Last?"

Mrs Last? Oh, yes. "Three, four weeks maybe."

The officer nodded, letting his eyes slide over the row of letters –szcz where Dasha was born, and handed back her passsport.

She was free to go and hang around the carousels, waiting for a suitcase that would probably turn up buried underneath three others, looking just like it.

*

Pink stood on tiptoe.

"You can't see anything over the top," he complained.

Asmodus looked at the clock for the first time in two minutes. "You have to be patient, angel. She's probably having some oaf paw through her suitcase right now, lusting after her dirty underwear."

Nancy's knees felt peculiar. That last orange one had been a mistake. She leaned against a trolley which ran forward in slow motion, and crashed into a barrier: a million faces turned round to stare, then turned back into a blur concentrated on the first arrivals from Paris. Nancy tried hard to concentrate too, but the people came by too fast. She gave up and watched Asmodus instead, ready to take her cue from his starting forward, smiling his wrap-around smile when Dasha finally came through the sliding doors.

*

It was a perfect day to be out in the boat, skimming up and down river, comparing the merits of different drinks at all the waterside pubs. Stéphane admitted cheerfully to herself that she was lazy, and her idea of viewing the wharf from the river had been a brilliant excuse for a day off. Still, the wharf would have to be looked at, because Martin was certain to ask about it, and because, Stéphane finished her drink and set off upriver towards Gabriel's, because she was cursed with a superstition about making her peace with buildings she was going to destroy.

She had heard somewhere that this one was haunted: on a mistier day she might have believed it. She might even have regretted that it was too late to save Gabriel's Wharf, wash the walls clean, wipe away the streaks of grey-green and rust running down from the windows. She cut the motor and let the boat drift close to the jetty, where there was a ring to tie up and rest.

Oh, she had been drinking too much. She reached out and felt the stonework; the place was rotting away, ugly and useless. She squinted upwards, following a crack that ran several feet from the roof: frost damage, probably. Strange how most of the windows still had glass in them. Some of the glass looked almost new, catching reflections of the clouds. In that one there was a cloud which looked like a face.

She looked around for a cloud in the shape of a face. There wasn't one. And when she looked back, the face in the window had gone.

She frowned and stared again, at all the windows. No more faces. "Ah ha," she said to herself in a quavering voice, "the ghost of old Gabriel is walking," but she didn't feel inclined to meet him. She reached up to slip the rope from its ring, then froze. A head popped out of the window just above her.

"Hello," Asmodus said.

Stéphane swallowed hard. "Hello."

"Were you looking for someone?"

She shook her head.

"No? Are you sure? Well then," Asmodus waved graciously in the direction of the creek. "It's nice here, isn't it? Do stay as long as you like."

He was about to pull his head back and go away when Stéphane lifted her hand, sharply. "Just a minute."

He leaned out again.

"You seem to be quite at home here," she remarked.

"Of course." He spread his arms wide. "I am the Essential Asmodus, Fantast in Abstract, and Empress of Gabriel's Wharf. Who are you?"

"Ah." Stéphane sat back and trailed her fingers in the water. She was beginning to enjoy herself. "I am the Architect Extraordinary, Fantast in Concrete, master of all I survey . . . though of course," she added casually, "I haven't come to survey your empire. Only to admire it."

Asmodus blinked. It was not going to be possible to frighten the lady away. What did she really want, sitting there so calmly in her boat, looking out across the river? Why don't you smile? he thought. Smile, like you did that day in the courtyard when the man kissed you.

"Don't you ever smile?" he asked, with a touch of slyness.

"Yes," she replied absently, "when I forget myself."

For a while she sat absorbed, considering the various possibilities of the situation. There was only one possibility which appealed to her, but it was risky. Still, her instinct told her Asmodus was harmless. She decided to trust her instinct.

"Essential Asmodus, will you let me come up and look around?"

"Extraordinary lady, I will show you around myself."

He threw out a rope-ladder for her to climb up, and offered his hand to help her over the sill. Such a light, frail creature. He would have to keep an eye on her. A very close eye indeed. At worst, he could prevent her seeing too much. At best, she might give herself away. If she had any sinister intention. Which was not evident, after all.

She coughed politely and he recollected himself. "Yes, well I suggest we begin in the courtyard and work up? If you come this way," he stepped over a broken floorboard and heaved open the gates of the loading bay, "this is the main door, solid iron. We don't use it much. Only for special guests. Be careful, the grand staircase is a little in need of repair. Give me your arm, it's quite safe, really."

They stepped out into the courtyard, which looked more of a mess than ever. Stéphane pointed to Pink's old van, still rusting away in its corner. "Is that yours too?"

Asmodus patted it. "This is Jane Austin, she works the winch."

"What winch?"

"When we find things in the river," he explained patiently, "we winch them up to the top. The rope goes through a pulley, then we fix one end to the van and drive it across the yard, so the other end gets pulled up, you see?"

"Sounds lethal."

Asmodus began to reassure her that it was quite safe, then realised that her attention had been caught by something else: she was staring past him up to the roof, her eyes narrowed in the sunlight, or in disbelief. He turned round and saw a row of silent figures, peering down over the parapet. Most of them were wearing funny hats.

The figures withdrew hurriedly and Stéphane turned back to Asmodus, raising her eyebrows.

"I may have forgotten to mention," he said, "that the Honourable Nancy Whitton is engaged in creating her latest videodrama here."

"Indeed." Something like amusement caught at Stéphane's expression, then vanished. "Have we seen everything in the courtyard now? Perhaps we could look inside."

He led her back through the main door and on into the upper storeys, doing his best to show her what they meant to him, these whitewashed rooms with their echoing iron pillars and arching windows; the serenity in the roughness of the massive stonework; grandeur of romanesque dimensions. The kittens, Nero and Caligula, followed them about, squeaking.

"This is the Vault of Loneliness," he said, opening the door of the cool-room where cheese had once been stored. "See, no windows. I come here when I want to be left alone. And up there, is the Torture Chamber. I don't know what all these rings and chains were for, really. You have to use your imagaination. If you come this way, we can take these stairs to the Singing Gallery."

Stéphane climbed the steps, slowly, up out of the shadows of chains, and through a hatch where the sunlight flared in from a score of windows stretching down a long, long room.

She stood still, and looked. And listened, almost forgetting to breathe.

The singing sound seemed to radiate out from the centre of the gallery and reflect itself from wall to wall, a shower of notes almost below the threshold of hearing. Stéphane thought about it, and then leaned out of a window to check her theory. She was wrong. There were no open pipes running underneath the floor.

Asmodus watched her, with his head on one side. She turned back to him, curiously, "Tell me the secret."

"I don't think anybody knows the secret. Maybe you'd have to take the wharf apart to find out."

A cloud drifted across the sun, and her eyes turned to the colour of iron: she felt tempted to tell him why she had come. He waited, but the moment passed.

They walked on up towards the roof, pausing to stare into the spiral grain-chute – The Black Hole, explained Asmodus and Stéphane had her hand scratched when she tried to prevent Nero from tottering too near the edge.

"The roof," said Asmodus grandly, "is our paradise. Come and see the river."

They shared the view of water, and boats, in silence until Asmodus ventured to ask Stéphane if he might know her name. He was surprised when she told him: he would never have known she wasn't English?

"I've lived here a long time." Stéphane remembered the warm, oil-smelling corridors of a ship sailing to somewhere called Southampton, her mother dressed in a golden gown covered with playing-cards, kissing her good-night and be good, underneath the porthole. Mummy's going to a fancy-dress ball. Without Daddy. Daddy the ambassador, who used to say he was descended from the Pompadour's husband, Le Normant d'Étioles.

Her memories were broken by a commotion in the courtyard. Nancy was screaming at her thespians not to carry their severed heads around like handbags. "This is supposed to be an orgy, right? not a poofters' tea-party. I told you, you got to be really wild, so that when the Tartar Prince comes out on the balcony and you all stop dead, like that, it's shattering, got it? Now then."

Stéphane and Asmodus grinned at each other, watching the progress of the orgy. Asmodus pointed out a walkway directly opposite them, which played the part of a balcony where the royal presence was to manifest itself. In a minute, Nancy would give a signal and Dasha, dressed up like a firebird, would step out to cut the orgy dead. Asmodus also warned Stéphane not to laugh, because Nancy's effects were never shattering in the way they were intended.

Stéphane didn't laugh. When the great moment came she only smiled, in the way Asmodus remembered. Lady, he thought, you've forgotten yourself.

Even Nancy would never have expected that.

The appearance of the Tartar Prince made Stéphane forget herself, the wharf project, Martin, and everything else which had seemed important only a few hours ago.

"Sometimes I worry about my daughter."

Adam looked up, expressing the appropriate sympathetic concern over Martin's daughter. Whenever Adam met Helen Geering, she treated him like a footman. These days she had a sort of job in an advertising agency run by one of Martin's friends. She was a spoiled brat.

"Nothing serious, I hope?" he prompted.

Martin smiled. "She doesn't seem to think so. She just said that she saw a man following her in the underground. Two or three times now."

Adam pulled at his moustache. He knew Helen had her licence taken away for dangerous driving, so now she had to go to work by tube like everyone else. It was difficult to make a tactful suggestion about that. He decided to sidestep the issue altogether.

"I wouldn't worry too much about it, Martin. After all, she's a very attractive girl, isn't she? You can't blame a man for following her, he's probably not a creep really, just normal."

Martin chuckled, true enough, and called for another drink. All the same, he thought it was a ridiculous idea for Helen to be working at all. His daughter didn't have to work. But her mother thought it would be good for her, "a maturing experience". Martin frowned. He didn't want Helen to experience ugly things. You have to protect the ones you love. He thought of Stéphane.

"Have you seen the plans for the wharf project lately?"

As it happened, Adam had sneaked a look at tham the day before. They were still terrible. He enthused about them, but thought Stéphane was a little over-awed by being given something so big to handle. "She's a perfectionist," he explained. "You know how women can be, it's difficult for her to see things as a whole. She'll get over it though," he added quickly, sensing that he had overstepped the mark. "All she needs is a bit of advice, you never have to give her the same advice twice. She's so bright, she frightens me."

"Me too." Martin looked over Adam's head, smiling. "And here she is." Both men stood up, offering Stéphane her choice of the empty seats between them. "Stéphane, you look very lovely this evening. Your partner was just saying the most flattering things about you."

"I wish he'd say them to me." Stéphane relaxed into her chair, and smiled up at the waiter who was part of the Friday evening ritual. Stéphane and Martin having supper in Martin's favourite restaurant. Sometimes with Adam. Always with Giles, that waiter.

"Stéphane, what will you drink?" Martin continued the ritual, comfortably. Giles leaned forward, waiting to be told to fetch madam's usual, a dry sherry.

"A Blue Lagoon, please," madam said idly, having decided that this Friday wasn't going to follow the usual routine.

"Good idea – and one for me," ordered Adam, wondering what on earth a Blue Lagoon was.

"Are you up to something?" Martin leaned over and put his hand on Stéphane's wrist. "Between us girls, what's a Blue Lagoon?"

"Us girls don't share all our secrets. Ask Adam. See if he'll tell you."

"Does Adam know all your secrets?"

Stéphane laughed. "He probably makes Blue Lagoons with gin and ink, don't you Adam? Otherwise, you can always use blue curaçao." She took the glass and gave it to Martin. "Try it. You might think it's a bit sweet, though."

Martin was puzzled, "But you don't like sweet things either?" and gave it back after one sip. It was too sweet, horribly sweet, and he buried himself in the menu, trying to forget the taste.

Stéphane continued to disturb him all through the meal: she wasn't her usual graceful self, following the conversation with intelligent agreement. Not that she could ever be aggressive, but she seemed to be out of tune, somehow, and it was making everyone feel uncomfortable. The talk drifted around to ghosts. One of Martin's friends had bought a haunted manor and then sold it again for half the price six months later because, Martin knew for a fact, Mrs Friend liked to run out and play with the stable-boys after dark. Although the friend would talk about the haunting in lurid detail as his reason for selling up, the details were different every time he described them.

"I stayed in a haunted house once," said Adam, "when I was a student."

"What did your ghost do?"

"I never saw her. She was supposed to be a nice ghost, very young and pretty, and she used to walk across one of the bedrooms and look out of the window. The strangest thing was, people said she floated along about a foot above the floor."

Martin was intrigued. Right, you sometimes heard about ghosts who did that. Did Adam's ghost always do that? Why? Adam knew why. He had got hold of some old plans, and found that the floors had been lowered in that part of the house. Ever since then, he had thought that ghosts were like a playback of something recorded in the fabric of the place. Otherwise, why would you get a distorted image when you altered the building's structure? There had to be a rational explanation for everything.

"Doesn't explain," Stéphane objected, "why some people see them and some people don't".

Adam turned on her. "Can you think of a better explanation? Incidentally," he added mildly, "isn't Gabriel's wharf supposed to be haunted?"

Stéphane put down her fork. He had promised her he wouldn't mention the wharf all evening. He'd done it on purpose. She made the best of it, and smiled radiantly.

"I didn't see any ghosts there."

"When I took you to see it?" Martin asked.

"No, I went back there yesterday, in Adam's boat. I told you."

"But you didn't go inside, did you? I thought you were only going to look at it from the river."

Stéphane shrugged. "When I got there, it seemed a good chance to have a look round, that's all. I wanted to get the feel of it."

"Stéphane, I don't like you going there by yourself. Those old buildings are dangerous. I don't want you breaking your neck. And another thing, what if you'd found a tramp there? I didn't want to frighten you, but when we were looking around that time I got the feeling someone was watching us."

Stéphane bowed her head, duly frightened, as though Martin or Adam might see Asmodus, the Vault of Loneliness, and the Singing Gallery, and the Prince of Xanadu, all betrayed in her expression. The Essential Asmodus had given her a glimpse of the Essential Wharf, a decayed shell where a few lunatics made up their own fairy-tales; a place where anything was possible, from breaking your neck to falling in love, or spinning silver dreams where you wished for things you'd never been taught to want. Martin wouldn't understand: if she told him about the squatters he would bring the demolition date forward, out of spite. No point in having a crisis of conscience over it. Let the fairy-tales live on a little longer, and come to an end in their own time. Stéphane laid her steak open down the middle, and watched a trickle of blood ooze out through the sauce. Then she looked up and entered light-headed into a new variation of the joyless game called hide-the-truth-from-Martin. As always, he made it easy for her.

"I didn't want to frighten you," he said again. "But don't look so worried, it was only my stupid imagination. Don't think about it any more. Just promise me one thing, don't go wandering round the wharf by yourself again, will you?"

"No," she said. "I won't explore it by myself."

*

When Adam finished eating, it often occurred to him that he didn't really enjoy meals with Martin and Stéphane. Then he would only stay long enough to do what was expected of him: offer Stéphane a lift home, so that she could refuse him and accept a lift with Martin instead. Adam yawned.

"Stéphane, can I offer you a lift home?"

"Thank you, but I came in my own car tonight."

Oh no, he thought. Don't keep changing the script, I hate you. None of us are any good at improvising.

"Goodnight, Adam."

"Thanks Martin, Stéphane. Goodnight."

Stéphane didn't need to improvise; she had worked it all out in advance. She looked very fragile as she sat in her car, kissing Martin through the window and gently insisting that she wanted to be by herself tonight. It was true, she reasoned, as she idled round the City a second time. If she hadn't really wanted to be by herself, it would have been too much to bear the hung way Martin stood watching her as she drove off. She would have turned back and gone with him.

The wharf was on her mind. The wharf, the wharf. The place would end up driving her mad. There would be no harm in going past it, just a look on her way home.

She put her foot down and took off in the direction of the river.

Quadrant Street, the wharf was in Quadrant Street. And it was all so dark. And empty. Quadrant Street. Not even the taxis came here at night. The warehouses were blind. No-one in their right minds came here at night, alone. Stéphane slowed down and groped for a cigarette, soothing the nightmare four-year old child inside her head. Gently, steady, gently. Just turn around and drive home nicely. One last little look down Quadrant Street, see? There's nothing to be afraid of.

Please God, no please God.

She trod on her brakes, staring. There was a fire. Unmistakeable, orange shadows flickering on the courtyard wall. Don't let it be happening. Drive away. No. The people. The people in there, trapped, burning. She wrenched the car round, peeling the tyres, screaming noises echoing up and down Quadrant Street.

Pink wandered over to the gate to see what the matter was.

Gravely he looked at her, sitting outside in her car, gaping at the courtyard scene, stunned.

The blaze roared up from a heap of packing-cases and driftwood, piled over a hole in the paving-stones. In and out of the firelight Asmodus went capering, playing a haphazard dance on a shabby accordion. He fumbled half the notes, and the ones that he managed to hit were out of tune to the point of senselessness. An eightsome reel in chaos flat minor, late twentieth-century style, molto approximato. As bandmaster, Asmodus had put on his tuxedo: a fluttering collection of plum-coloured velvet rags tied together round his neck with an enormous wing-collar, picked out by the flames in two high-pointed shadows darting around the walls. The Honourable Nancy was perched on an oildrum with her back to him, busy thrusting long wires into the bottom of the fire. In the corner another figure sat as shadow audience, unmoving and unmoved, on an orange-box.

Stéphane let down her window, took a deep breath, and astonished Pink with a torrent of abuse. The shadow on the orange-box looked round and stood up, glad of the diversion. Pink appealed to it for help.

"I can't understand what she's saying. Is it French, Dasha, you

24

understand French don't you? What's she so upset about?"

"I think," Dasha decided, "she's upset because she thought the wharf was on fire."

"How very touching." Asmodus appeared beside the window, beaming. "To see someone who cares so deeply about my empire." He peered in. "Hello again, Fantast in Concrete. So glad you could come to our party."

Stéphane found a cigarette and lit it, twice, because her hands were trembling. Pink shrugged at Dasha and they both slid away, like cowards, leaving Asmodus to do his duty as host.

"Well," he said, "it's nice here, isn't it?"

Stéphane was silent.

"Do stay as long as you like. We must get to know each other better, then I won't have to keep repeating myself. You'll excuse me now, I mustn't neglect my other guests."

Left alone, Stéphane slumped back in her seat, willing her brain to start moving again. Her brain needed a drink. It was flushing hot and cold with waves of mortification. She had made such a fool of herself.

"Try and drink this." It was Dasha back outside, holding a glass. "Drink it, it's good. You'll feel better." She crouched down beside the window, resting her chin on her arms, glancing down to see if Stéphane's hands were still shaking. "Take your time," she added calmly. "Have as much as you want. I brought the bottle with me. And I stole a mushroom too." Triumphantly, she produced a tiny burnt mushroom and dangled it outside the window. "That's Nancy over there, she's the expert for doing burnt mushrooms."

Stéphane recoiled. What sort of mushrooms were they?

Dasha looked thoughtful. "I can't remember just what she calls them . . . she got a book about them, she was telling us. She has to get up at dawn to look for them, and when she finds one she says 'OM' over a pair of scissors, or something, then she throws a few yarrow sticks, no, I got that wrong, the yarrow sticks are when she consults the oracle, anyway, the mushrooms. She creeps us behind them and snips them off when they're not looking. She says it's best to take them before you make love, so I don't know why she's wasting them on us, really. Why don't you try a bit?"

"I might." Stéphane grinned suddenly, thinking of Eve in the Garden of Eden, wondering if Dasha had a forked tongue. Temptation and more temptation, as easy and graceful as temptation should be.

"I'll let you share this one," Dasha said, "if you come in and sit by the fire."

Stéphane pretended to think about it.

"If you don't stay," Dasha went on smoothly, "Nancy will be very unhappy."

"Why Nancy?"

"Because she noticed you watching her orgy yesterday and Asmodus told her you were in raptures about it."

"Did you see me?"

"Yes, I saw you. So stay this time, don't run away." Dasha held out the mushroom.

Stéphane lifted up her head and bit the stalk off.

Dasha shifted uncomfortably, and stood up, dropping the rest of the mushroom into her own mouth. "It's cold here. Come over to the fire now, and get warm." Her hand came through the window and rested on Stéphane's shoulder. "Will you?"

"If you help me."

"Give me your hand." Dasha stood back, holding out both her arms to lift Stéphane up. "Arise, Concrete Fantast".

"Lead on, Tartar Prince."

In the courtyard, the flames flared up, whirled into sparks by the breeze. Stéphane stood for a long moment, warming her hands and staring through the heart of the fire, where a piece of driftwood crumbled in and turned to gold.

*

"Asmodus?" Nancy waved a bare wire over the top of the fire. "Was it you?"

"Me what, my love?"

"Stealing my mushrooms."

"Uh, probably. I couldn't wait for wonderful things to start happening." Asmodus beamed at her, and wondered whether Dasha had been very wise to feed Stéphane one of those things. But then, Nancy's things never had much effect. He wished they would. He sighed and glanced over at Stéphane, sitting very properly on an orange-box, and Dasha, lounging on a blanket by her side. What timewasters, women. And Pink was cramping their style: he had trotted over to chat to them, no doubt so they wouldn't feel left out of things. So instead of absorbing themselves in touching conversations, they all looked as though they were keeping up a polite discussion.

They were trying to make sense of Nancy's videodrama. Stéphane wanted to know what scenes Dasha had done.

"Let's see." Dasha leaned back on her elbow and reflected. "There was the orgy, that you saw yesterday, and then there was a big hairy guy in chains, with a bow in his hair, he walked up and down in front of me on his knees. And another guy called Sabrina and his group . . . Sabrina Slink and Scrubbers? Something like that. They did a couple of numbers."

"What for?"

"To entertain me, I guess. Court entertainers at Xanadu. Kubla Khan must be turning in his grave."

Pink sniggered, and called across the fire. "Nancy, tell us something."

Nancy winkled out a wire and studied the blob on the end. "These one's aren't ready yet."

"Not the mushrooms. Xanadu."

"What's that?"

"Xanadu! Stéphane wants to know all about it!"

Asmodus kept a watchful eye on the proceedings, ready to play peacemaker if anyone upset Nancy by asking something silly, like what the story line was. At first, all went well. Nancy settled into relating how she had heard a voice telling her that the time of Word was past, and that henceforth all videodramas should be wordless.

'It's funny, a voice telling you that," Pink said, wonderingly.

"A voice, a vision, what does it matter? It's what the message was that's important."

Asmodus passed his hands over his eyes. Pink had gone on to commit the unforgiveable. He had dared to ask Nancy what Xanadu was about.

"How should I know what it's about?" Nancy shrieked, scornfully. "You just do it, and see what happens. Does it have to be *about* something?"

Dasha gazed up at her, unconcerned.

Pink looked as though he wanted to burst into tears.

"Isn't there a script?" Stéphane asked in a weak voice. "An outline?"

Scripts? Outlines? Nancy stared at her in horror, and Asmodus decided it was time to intervene. Of course, nobody expected anything so cramping as a *structure,* but they were just curious to know where Nancy's idea had come from? She had such marvellous ideas. Nancy agreed. Actually, she had come across the idea in a book of Chinese fairy-tales.

"My mother gave me a basket of Chinese games once," said Pink, dreamily. Nancy glared at him. "She found it in the market," he went on, "but all the instructions were in Chinese. So I never knew how to play them."

"Don't mind him, Nancy, he's out of his brains. Go on. You were saying, once upon a time?"

Nancy didn't answer.

"Maybe," Dasha said, "the fairy-tales were all in Chinese too."

Nancy opened her mouth to say something spiteful, then changed her mind and went back to tending the mushrooms, while Asmodus dragged Pink away into a corner to stop him doing any more harm.

"You see how it is." Dasha scrambled to her knees and whispered over Stéphane's shoulder. "You're not supposed to laugh. Some of us can't help asking silly questions."

Stéphane leaned back, closing her eyes to the sky, rocked by the sweet, exciting smell of a strange skin.

"Listen, my loves!" Asmodus commanded their attention, holding up the roundabout horse by one leg. "The time has come for us all to wish. Do we wish on a star? No. Do we wish on a ring? No! Do we wish on the roundabout horse? Yes!"

He lifted the horse above his head and flung it into the flames. Wishes are made in heaven: carry them back there, roundabout horse, as they fall due.

Pink cheered. There was nothing else for him to do. All that dragging the horse out of the river, and washing it in the bath. All gone up in smoke.

"Fame and fortune!" Nancy called out.

"Shush, Nancy, you're not supposed to say it out loud."

"Have another drink, everybody."

"Look, it's melting."

The horse's neck twisted as it settled onto a glittering bed of crossed planks, sinking down through the heat haze, undulating, languidly opening up its belly, wider and wider as the flames reached inside.

"Did we make the same wish?" Dasha put her arms around Stéphane's shoulders. "Kiss and tell."

"Your silly question. Is your blanket comfortable?"

"And yours. Lie down and see."

Asmodus picked up his accordion and began singing softly to himself.

"The water is wide, I cannot cross o'er,
And neither have I wings to fly . . . ."

Who needs wings? Dasha thought, drawing the blanket around herself and Stéphane; a cloak to fold in some darker warmth away from the scorching flicker of the bonfire, warmth filled with soaring, floating enchantments.

"O love is fine, and love is blind,
And love's a jewel, when it is new;
But when it is old, it groweth cold,
And fades away, like morning dew."

So much for love. Dasha's eyes rested gently on Stéphane's smile, and she shook her head. "Asmodus?"

"Speak."

Dasha twisted round to protest. "Do you have to sing miserable songs? Can't you sing something else?"

"What do you suggest?"

"I don't know . . . football songs, nursery rhymes, anything."

"Why don't you tell us a story?" Nancy demanded.

"A lullaby," murmured Pink, who could hardly keep his eyes open.

"Nursery-rhymes, and fairy-tales, and lullabies." Hollow with the courtyard echo, Asmodus' voice sounded in Stéphane's drowsing mind. "My subjects clamour to be entertained. Listen to yourselves. You're all asleep."

Stéphane dreamed that she was leading Asmodus through a

forest. She knew the forest so well that she must have planted the trees herself: arranged in neat rows, so high and thick that they shut out the wind and the rain. Asmodus was looking for flowers. She felt annoyed at him for pestering her about the flowers. She used to grow them, she ran about looking . . . but they were old; shrivelled and faded. "Didn't you think to plant new ones?" he accused her, "instead of all these trees?" And his question made her feel a terrible sense of regret, something not cared about and lost, so that she howled as though nothing would comfort her.

She awoke silently, her eyes sticky with tears, and Dasha watching her with a curious expression.

"Don't be sad," Dasha said. "It was only a dream."

"Only a dream," Asmodus repeated, from the shadows. He unstrapped his accordion and stretched, catching sight of Nero's fluffy outline on the wall beside the gate. The kitten might have been crouching there all night, only taking shape as the colour of the sky changed. Asmodus bowed to the dawn.

"Well," he said, "we can't stay here all day. Get up! It's such a shame to wake you, though. How pretty Nancy looks with her mouth open." Sentimentally he smoothed Pink's hair. "Time to climb the iron ladder, angel."

Silence.

In the uncertain light, the walls around him seemed to swell and recede, as though the wharf itself were breathing.

Asmodus contemplated Stéphane, huddled in her blanket. And what shall we do with her? he pondered.

He jumped at the sound of the car starting up. Dasha leaned out of the window and called across to him. "Move! I'm coming in."

"Are we all going for a dawn drive?" he asked brightly.

"Not today." Dasha got out and knelt down beside Stéphane. "You don't have to wake up yet. I'll take you home, if you want."

Asmodus sighed over Dasha's selfishness. He would have liked to go for a dawn drive. But Dasha, thoughtless creature, only wanted to go out and play tender lovers in somebody else's wendy-house.

*

Stéphane edged out of the bedclothes and stretched into a patch of sun underneath the skylight. The arm underneath her shoulders woke up and wound a sheet around itself, finding nothing.

"Where are you?" Dasha asked, hazily.

"Watching the clouds go by."

"Mmm."

Stéphane unwound the arm gently and sat up to think. Martin, that was the problem, Martin on Sundays. One day when he hadn't seen her for two weeks he had felt guilty and made a new decree: henceforth all his Sundays were devoted to her; and behold, he had gone forth to buy a cottage, where he could exercise his devotion during the intervals of exercising his muscles in healthy rustic activities. She shook herself. It wasn't fair to make fun of him: he was kind. But all his fantasies were so predictable. Country cottages, good grief. Next summer it would probably be a yacht. She bet herself a fiver it would be a yacht.

"Have you worked us all out yet?"

"At the wharf?" Stéphane looked down, and forgot about Martin. "No, of course not. That's why I can't keep away from you."

"Would you have stayed last night, if I hadn't given you that drink?"

"Oh, I expect so . . . but your being there had something to do with it, probably."

"Even when I started babbling about mushrooms?"

Stéphane protested: it wasn't babble.

"Yes it was, I couldn't stand listening to myself half the time. I didn't want to talk about mushrooms at all really, what I wanted to do was say fascinating things in a deep, cool voice, so that . . ."

Stéphane made a sound that could have been either a groan or a laugh; she wasn't sure herself which it was. Dasha did have a forked tongue. She was a serpent. "All you really care about," Stéphane said, "is your own pleasure. Sensual beast."

"Once or twice I think about yours as well."

"Don't, will you?" Stéphane slid out of Dasha's reach and sat on the edge of the bed, hugging herself.

Dasha dropped her hands in astonishment, puzzled and a little hurt. "Don't what?"

"Don't make me want to lie here with you all day. You'll make me die." There was a shine of sweat all over Stéphane's body, and her face had gone pale, even though she was smiling. "What are you doing to me?" she asked, staring into Dasha's eyes with mock intensity. "I want so much to save myself for you."

"It's a bit late for that, isn't it?"

"You don't know what I've got in mind for tonight."

Dasha grumbled that it would make her brain hurt, thinking up things to keep her going till then. She stretched out and put her hands behind her head, smiling to herself. She wanted to know if Stéphane would come back with her to the wharf tomorrow.

It took Stéphane a long time to answer. No, not tomorrow. There was something else she had to do.

"Is it so bad?" Dasha sat up, laughing. "You got a secret lover who sweeps you away on Sundays, or what?"

"That's right."

Dasha's eyes opened wide. "Not really?"

"Really. Truly."

"How clever of me to guess." Dasha thought about it. "It doesn't matter," she decided at last. "I've got a secret lover in Paris too, only I don't have to see her. Because she's there and I'm here. I'd rather be here."

"So would I." Stéphane stretched and strolled about the room, looking for a towel. "So would I." She turned on the shower. "Tell me about your secret lover."

"She writes songs. You know what French songs are like." Dasha hummed over a tuneless dirge, puncuated by stabs of passion.

"How do the words go?"

"Usual thing." Dasha roughed out the first three verses: when you begged me to share your life, your home; when you started asking me for rent; when you threw my things out in the street . . . "Want me to go on?"

"No, I think I've got the idea. Can you pass me that towel?"

"What about your secret lover?"

"He's not as interesting as yours. He doesn't write songs, he only makes money."

"Don't knock money, it's a fine thing." Dasha patted Stéphane's back dry, and took over the shower. "He, did you say?"

"I'm not going to marry him, if that's what you mean."

"But my love," Dasha's voice took on the soft drawl of the Empress of Gabriel's Wharf. "Why shouldn't you be married to him? I myself am married. I'm married to Asmodus, great Queen of the Night."

Stéphane burst out laughing and walked away. "You don't believe me," Dasha called out, "so what does being married matter? Forget it."

Stéphane couldn't forget it. The whole idea of Dasha being married to Asmodus was so idiotic it made her smile, every time she thought about it. The story only came out in disjointed scraps, between gusts of laughter when they were sitting outside on the grass: the Immigration Office, the Great Art Gallery Squat, the man from the Social Security who didn't believe the marriage either. Dasha found a frilly frock in a skip, and left it about the place to prove her wifely femininity when the man from the Social Security came round snooping. He wasn't fooled, poor guy. He probably thought the frock belonged to Asmodus.

"Will you tell me something now?" Dasha asked, after they'd finished laughing.

"Something silly?"

"Could be. Why does Asmodus call you a Fantast?"

Stéphane explained about her first meeting with Asmodus. It was his word, she'd only copied it, that was all: she didn't even know what a Fantast was.

"I knew it. I knew you were only a pretend Fantast." Dasha sucked at her teeth, severely. "But it's not your fault. If you stay around the wharf long enough, you'll probably turn into a real one. Do you want to, though? I wonder."

"If you want to be one, does it mean you have to act like Asmodus?"

"By no means." The lines around Dasha's lips deepened into a half-smile, while she concentrated her thoughts. "There aren't any set rules for being a Fantast, that's the whole point about them. But maybe you could say they spend their lives improvising round whatever seems real to them, not following patterns other people worked out."

"Your word?"

"No, I got it from an English guy I met in New York. Someone who knew Asmodus."

Stéphane had been to New York, too. They exchanged memories of it for a while: clouds by day on top of the World Trade Center; Manhattan by night, looking like rocks heaped on the shore, flecked with fool's gold. Chinatown. The Statue of Liberty. Stéphane had only gone as a visitor. Dasha had lived there two years, yin-ed and yang-ed her way through it all and enjoyed it, up to a point. But she preferred Paris. "The wharf reminds me of it sometimes, when the tourists go up and down the river. Guess the first thing I did, when I got to Paris. Took a boat trip all the way round."

Dasha shook her head, recalling the umpteen thousand tons of girders and millions of bolts they said made up the Eiffel Tower, and how many people you could cram inside Notre-Dame: Our Lady of Paris, nine hundred years of history and still young. "I don't know anything. I was sitting there in this glass boat, thinking what a romantic exile I was, and then you know what I saw? What are you laughing again for? At me?" Dasha looked suspicious, in a good-humoured way. "You think I'm funny, is that what you think?"

"I don't know . . . you just sounded nice, when you said that. I'm not laughing at you. Don't tell me what you saw, let me think for a moment." Stéphane stretched out for a blade of grass and put it between her teeth, crinkling her eyes against the sunset. When she was small she used to walk beside the Seine every day, on her way to some grim school or other. Fragments of the time came back to her, slowly: the shape of a lamp-post, the face of an old woman who used to sell magazines. But the river?

Recognition. She caught her breath in surprise, or even delight. Of course, it was obvious. "Yes, I know now! I've got it." She put her hand on Dasha's wrist, urgently. "The Statue of Liberty, wasn't it that? The little one, where all the boats turn round?"

"Yes, yes yes yes!" Dasha rolled over on her back, reaching up to touch Stéphane's face, with a sense of wonder that she was there, that she was alive, that they existed together and the source of their feeling was in each other, not in themselves.

She couldn't catch the moment. It slipped away, with a kind of radiant sadness that partings sometimes gave.

Stéphane shivered. "I can hardly see you anymore, it's getting so dark. Come back inside, it's warmer there. I feel closer to you in the light. By the fire."

*

Martin swung his axe above his head, then let is sweep down, with a shock that almost jolted his arms out of their sockets and just missed his foot. But the log split cleanly along the middle, that was good. He had picked out all the rotten ones to chop first. Only him and Stéphane, together in their Sunday cottage in the country, sweet with the sound of church bells. Heaven.

He leaned on the shaft of his axe and gazed across at her, swinging in the hammock, sipping a mug of tea and unpicking a swiss roll. He thought he had never seen her look so lovely and so alive.

"How the fresh air suits you," he said.

She carried on swinging, considering the joys of life in the country with Martin. An ant swimming in her tea; a clicking sound on the path, as a thrush hopped up and down bashing the insides out of a snail. She had spent most of the weekend on her back, looking up at the sky.

"I feel like Marie Antoinette playing at shepherdesses," she said carelessly, stretching out her foot to give the hammock another shove. "Let them eat cake."

She threw him a piece of swiss roll.

"I don't want you to get cold, though," he went on. "Are you alright there?"

"Yes, sir. Carry on with your chopping."

"Is your car still out the front? I'll get that blanket you keep on the back seat."

"Thanks. It's not locked."

She closed her eyes and drifted into some kind of daydream, not one with any beginning or end, just a torso of sensations. The sight, sound, smell, taste and touch of Dasha.

"Stéphane!"

She jumped. Martin was standing beside her, trailing the blanket, with a worried look on his face. She blinked at him. "What's the matter?"

"Your car! I've just seen your car."

Oh yes, that. Stéphane nearly laughed out loud when she thought of her car. It needed a new bumper, and a new wing, and a new door. The result of trying to outdo Dasha in a game of French Driver Fantast. She reached up and patted Martin's face.

"Don't look so worried, I only caught a tree, I didn't hurt anyone. Isn't it funny, how little accidents can do so much damage? I haven't had time to get it fixed yet."

Uncertain, he shifted his feet while he stayed by the hammock, gazing down. But she always looked after her car so carefully: it wasn't like her, driving into trees and then laughing about it. There were times when he found it very hard to belive that he was coming any closer to her. Since his idea of the wharf project, he'd often wished himself into thinking he knew her better – usually when he'd had a few drinks – but the suspicion was there: whatever she might have been before, she'd changed since she began working on the wharf, and he understood less about her than ever. Liveliness was one thing. He loved her most when she was lively, but doing that to her car was more like wildness. Disturbing. Like a challenge, it excited him.

On impulse, he dragged a little wooden chair over to the hammock and straddled it, staring at her intently over the back. Expressionless, she returned his stare.

He picked up the blanket and drew it over her, taking care to cover the gaping neckline of her shirt. It kept distracting his thoughts. What did he want to tell her?

He summoned up all his feelings of tenderness and commitment, and struggled to pour them into what he said at last: "I do love you."

He knew it didn't sound as he wanted. It sounded fawning and sentimental. Servile.

"So do I." A formula reply, blighted by a touch of desperation.

He stretched out his hand and rocked the hammock for her, wondering if other people found it difficult to talk about what they felt. Not poets, or people like that, artists. Just ordinary people. Ordinary people very likely didn't have any problem: they had more time for this sort of thing than he did. Perhaps even poets didn't do any better than ordinary people, when they had to make do with reality. Flesh and blood. Martin took his hand away from the hammock and looked up at the clouds: the sky was all clouds now. "It'll be winter soon."

He decided that it was time to talk about safer things. "I've been thinking about next summer." His voice brightened, eager with some delight he'd been clutching to himself for days. "Guess what I've been thinking about? Something you'll like."

She cleared her throat, resolving to take him seriously; he didn't deserve to be made fun of. She tried to look as though she were really thinking. When the time was up she stopped furrowing her brow and said, with interest, "No, I give in. What?"

"A yacht!" he said triumphantly.

She couldn't help laughing. It wasn't much of a laugh really, more a chuckle. The sight of his bewildered face reminded her to explain.

"I bet myself a fiver that you'd – that you would . . . think of something amazing to do next summer. I know you, you see? how restless you are. My eagle."

"I like it when you call me that. You know about boats, don't you? You borrow Adam's. Tell me what you really think."

"I think it's a wonderful idea."

"I knew you would." He said it dreamily, imagining himself as commander at the tiller, staring unflinching at tidal waves towering up to the sky, riding over them into the salty vastness, skirting vicious rocks by a hair's breadth. The other yachtsmen a vague chorus to applaud his daring and provide a background glow in the snug afterwards, among the trophies. And Stéphane stretched out on the deck in the sun, with no clothes on.

"How d'you think I'd look in a peaked cap?" she asked. "With lots of gold tinsel all over it."

"Irresistible. But not too much tinsel, it wouldn't suit you. Not as much as me."

She pretended to sulk about that. He tickled her, enjoying her shrieks and wriggles, her imploring him to stop, he could have as much tinsel as he liked, she wouldn't have any, any at all.

"Listen," he said suddenly, freezing with his hand in the air. "Can you hear it?"

The call of a hunting horn, carried back across the fields. Stéphane strained to catch it, the sound of heroes who lost themselves in sinister forests, always in pursuit of fabulous creatures which eluded them.

Martin's eyes clouded with a different idea, the power of mounting astride a horse, mastering it and riding it into the ground.

He bent over Stéphane and whispered something in her ear. While his head was down, he couldn't see the listless expression that came over her face. The expression had disappeared by the time he straightened up, to be replaced by one more appropriate.

"Not here!" she objected. "What if someone sees us?"

"No-one's going to see us."

After all the times he must have kissed her, why was it that he still tasted like a stranger? "Martin! You can't get in here! Get off! You'll break it." The hammock swayed, crazily, nearly tipping them out onto the ground.

"Of course it won't break. Can't you do something with this blanket? It's all prickly. You know I can't stand prickly things."

"Let's get out. On the ground. It's not safe in here."

Martin didn't like the idea of the ground. Too cold. Very uncomfortable to the sensitivities. No more talking now, just feel the hammock rocking.

*

Even Dasha, Asmodus admitted reluctantly, couldn't entirely solve the problem of boring Sundays. He sat on a cushion behind her, pretending to write; Pink had placed her on the throne nearest the window, and was trying to sketch her profile. When Pink drew from models he did it dutifully, as something that was good for him, knowing that afterwards he would feel much better for having put Still Life away in a cupboard. Studied in the grey river-light, Dasha's expression defeated him: dark delicate, clear lines, too many reasons for each thought, glowing nights and harsh days. It's only a face, for heaven's sake. He grunted and scribbled in the edges of her hair.

Dasha twitched. "Am I boring you?"

"No, I'm boring myself. I can't decide the best way to do it. Perhaps if you talked to Asmodus for a bit, it would help me. I think it would."

"What shall we talk about, my love?" Asmodus closed his notebook, carefully.

"Why don't you tell us what you're writing?"

"I don't tell you because if I could, there wouldn't be any need to write it, would there?"

Dasha shrugged. "Don't bother, just strap on another claw to scratch me with. Your turn to think of something to talk about."

"Good." Asmodus sat up and stretched out his legs. "I have something serious to ask you."

"Oh really?"

"Really. I've been looking at these." From the window-sill, he took down a folio of slides and propped it against his knee, pausing for effect before delivering his judgement. "They're so beautifully done. As always. What I want to know is, why have you been wasting so much time over things like this?"

He waved his hand over a set of flowers and trees in various stages of decay. A sycamore with half its trunk burnt away, a sunflower hanging towards its roots, gnawed by a swarm of beetles, brilliant parasites and deformed hosts. "Or these?" accused Asmodus, turning over the page. A series of table-tops showing plates of half-eaten meals: the best bits picked out and the rest left.

Dasha scratched her lip. "Don't you like them? I thought they were romantic."

"I think they're morbid. And trivial."

Pink cringed into his corner, remembering Dasha's reputation for throwing things. Sometimes Asmodus deserved to have things thrown at him. But Dasha's reply was quite restrained, almost kind:

"Maybe that's how I think romance should look."

Pink swept his pencil in a thin slash around Dasha's jawline. "The trouble with romance," he decided, "is that it pretends people don't go to the toilet . . . Now I've got it. Don't stop laughing, you're much easier to draw when you laugh."

Asmodus folded up his legs, muttering something sour about toilets, and dragged his typewriter into position. "Your latest lover, I suppose, doesn't have a silly romantic thought in her head."

"My latest lover has a head, period."

Asmodus wound a sheet of paper through the roller and picked at the Y key, to see if it was still sticking. "There's no need to snap at me, just because she hasn't got time to play with you today."

Dasha's eyes glittered. It was a look that Asmodus remembered very well, as belonging to the more dangerous moments in his fleeting experience of married life. He had hurt her, and he regretted it.

"That's right," she said irritably. "She plays with someone else on Sundays. You expect me to hang around her back door with a ball under my arm, or what?"

"Of course not, my love. You've both got your own lives to lead, as you say. I'm only too glad that we can have you all to ourselves at least one day a week." The Y caught a bunch of spindly arms that jumped up and flopped randomly on the paper. "How you've changed since you met her," he went on, with insidious wistfulness. "Sometimes I think you don't even like us anymore. You only seem to be really happy when you're with her. Does she make you happy?"

"Oh, Asmodus, don't. Don't start on that used, abused, and thrown away stuff. Just don't start."

Asmodus raised his eyebrows. "You seem to be picking up one of her bad habits," he observed. "Not answering questions properly. Let me put it another way. Do you make her happy?"

"No, I don't think so. Not always."

Asmodus folded his hands in his lap and put his head on one side.

"She hides things," Dasha explained. "Or she doesn't always tell me the truth about herself. I don't know. It's just a feeling I get sometimes. Like the other day, when I asked her why she came here in the first place, she looked at me as though I'd touched a bruise, or something."

"And she didn't tell you?"

"I didn't ask her again."

My dear child, Asmodus thought, it's not difficult. She's an architect, and this place has the best river-view you've ever seen in London. She didn't come only for that, still . . . she nearly told me once, the first day she came here. Then she saw you, and now she doesn't even want to think about the end of the wharf, for your sake. That's sad, but it's nobody's fault.

He looked up, smiling brightly. "You women are so secretive.

Or you think you are. Why worry about it? Why not just get on and enjoy each other, little mysteries and all? Without brooding over what's true and what isn't."

"You're such a dreamer, Asmodus." Dasha dropped her head, then remembered that Pink was still struggling over his portrait. She adjusted the curve of her neck, carefully. "Why are you such a dreamer? Mm? Why do you think that is?"

"And what's the matter with you? Just because I hint, only hint, mind you, that love affairs are more fun when you don't go dragging *truth* into them, for heaven's sake. Don't be so demanding."

She favoured him with a look of bored amusement. "Didn't you tell me that once before, when you were going on about the Illusion of Self? That time Pink was trying to paint the inside of his brains, something like that?"

Pink hunched over his drawing and stuck his tongue out.

Asmodus ignored them both. "Who wants the truth anyway? People are much happier if you tell them what they want to hear."

Dasha smiled to herself, catching the bitter inflexion of one who spent his life pondering over great truths and then expounding them in pamphlets that nobody wanted to read. "When I first came to London," she said slowly, "I spent half my time wandering round in circles getting lost. You know why? Because when I asked people for directions and they didn't have any idea, they'd much rather pretend they did, and just make something up, so's not to disappoint me. Even if they sent me off in the opposite direction."

"I don't suppose . . . ."

". . . and it's the same with people. How can you get near them if they only tell you what they think you want to hear? You don't have to make the truth into some great ultimate revelation, listen to me will you just listen, full of moral meaning, and all that. It isn't, not to me. It's just something you need to know so you don't spend your time running round some waste-ground where you never wanted to be in the first place." She took a deep breath. "You listening to me, Merlin? Or are you just casting spells to shut me up?"

Asmodus beamed, as though with pleasure at some private joke.

"Do you know, your style's just as crude as it was when you left me? Evidently no-one else has managed to polish you up any more than I could, I'm delighted to see."

"That's right, you flatter yourself. Tell us what an aristocrat you turned me into." Dasha grinned back at him. "Go on. You do that. Tell us how tall, dark and handsome I am. We all want to hear that."

"You know perfectly well how tall, how dark, and how handsome you are. You take loving photographs of yourself often enough. You don't need me to bolster up your illusions. You're vain, and shallow, and completely beyond redemption."

Dasha snorted. Pink looked up, anxiously. "You're not quarrelling, are you?" he asked.

Asmodus stared in Pink's direction, with a far-away expression in his eyes. "No, angel, we weren't quarrelling, we were just being nostalgic, weren't we? Reminding ourselves how the Great Art Gallery Squat used to ring with our innocent screams." He rubbed the side of his face, frowning, and turned back to Dasha. "There was something I wanted to ask you, just now, but I forget, no, I remember what it was. Don't answer if you don't want to."

"Go on then, ask me. What is it?"

"Will you tell me what makes this Stéphane of yours so different from all the others?"

"I don't have lots of women, Asmodus. That's just your fantasy. I love her, that's all. I love her all the time."

"Even when she's hiding things?"

"Even then."

"Even when she's trying to nag you into being what *she* wants?"

"She never does that. Not ever."

"Well then, that's what makes her different."

Pink gave a sweet smile. "Perhaps she wants you exactly as you are," he said, fatuously. "There, I've finished. As soon as you started talking about her, it all came right. Do you think she'll like it?"

Asmodus reached out and took the sketch. It was superb, as true as Dasha's own photographs of herself.

"I think she'll like it very much," he said cautiously, because it would never do to turn Pink's head with lavish praise. He handed the drawing to Dasha, and went back to his typewriter.

"Asmodus?" Dasha's voice was tight, as though she was expecting to hear some ghastly confession.

"Yes, my love."

"Do you know why she came here in the first place?"

Asmodus tapped away a bit more. "I should think," he mused, "that when she came here, she was looking for you, without wanting to."

"How can you know that?"

Asmodus slid the paper out of his typewriter and studied the smattering of half-formed letters. "I know," he said gently, "because I dreamed her for you."

"Is that what you did." She reached back and stroked her fingers down his beard. "How is it we sometimes have the same dreams?"

"Not quite. Your dream ends differently from mine."

*

By some magic, the wharf had been clad in shimmering tinfoil splendour. Or part of it had. Stéphane paused in the gateway, wide-eyed, staring at the west face. Broad strips of foil had been plastered over it, glinting behind the winch contraption. She shook her head, admiringly. The effect was impressive.

"Fantast!" A joyful shout from the opposite direction. Dasha was standing on the royal balcony, calling down to her.

Stéphane ran across the courtyard and began the long climb up the fire-escape to the balcony, lifting her head as often as she dared, to smile at Dasha clambering down. They met part-way on a platform, reaching out their arms to draw each other into a long, fierce hug.

The platform rocked and groaned, as though it would twist away from the wall and fling them both back down onto the paving-stones. Dasha put out a hand to grasp the stanchion and steady the rocking. "Too much passion," she said lightly, "can be dangerous."

"But not fatal?" Stéphane wondered at herself for not feeling afraid.

"No, not fatal. It's quite safe, really. I've gone up and down it dozens of times, with Nancy screaming at me and everything, and it hasn't given way yet." Dasha started back up the steps, regally slow and upright, in a demonstration of the Tartar Prince's walk. "Come on, we'll go in by the balcony, d'you know where it leads?" She reached back for Stéphane's hand. "You tired already?"

They paused for breath on the walkway, taking in the view of the sheer silver wall opposite. "Behold Xanadu," Dasha said. "I think."

Xanadu had been built yesterday, in a burst of horrifying activity. The thespians clinging to the winch, Jane Austin jerking and grinding backwards and forwards across the courtyard, Pink hunched grimly over the steering-wheel, Nancy poking her camera at everybody, shrilling instructions over the frantic wails of extras about to fall to their deaths. "They'll be carrying on this afternoon. Nancy told everyone to get up early, about three o'clock, I guess. It'll be hell." Dasha struck a tragic attitude. "So we only have a few brief hours together, darlng. Whatever shall we do?"

"You going to play our tune now, or what?" Stéphane drawled back.

Dasha laughed at her, stooping down to unlatch the half-doors at the end of the balcony. "This way, ma'am." She threw the doors open and they stepped into the room Stéphane loved most of all: the Singing Gallery.

"Ah." Stéphane leaned against the wall, head on one side, to catch its music. But there was none. The Gallery wasn't singing; the drifts of sunshine were thick with dust and silence.

"What's wrong?" she asked, bewildered.

"Pardon me?"

"Why's the singing stopped?"

Oh, the sound. Dasha smiled suddenly, understanding what Stéphane meant. But the Gallery didn't always sing, only some days. Had it serenaded Stéphane every time until now?

"Never mind," Dasha said. "It's only asleep. We'll come back another day, when it wakes up." She pulled open a casement and leaned out. "But the river's as . . ." she stopped, choking back a snigger. "Want to see something funny? Come and look at this."

Four storeys below was the jetty where Stéphane had arrived in Adam's boat, and floating beside the jetty now was a dinghy; Pink straining at the oars and Asmodus arranged serenely in the prow, nose pointed towards the open river. Looking at the stern, Stéphane could see the dinghy's name, Trio, painted in gothic gold letters six inches high. Then she noticed what Dasha had seen: a taut rope vibrating, shaking a cluster of drips and splashes into the air. Trio was still tied to the mooring-ring.

A second later, Pink had realised his mistake and crawled over to slip the rope, looking round furtively to see if Asmodus had noticed. But Asmodus continued gazing riverwards with the same serenity of expression, undisturbed as the boat shot out through the creek.

"Come in quick, they might look up."

The two spectators fell back into the Gallery, giggling, crouching down underneath the window, touching their heads together with delight and rocking around in the dust. Dust and sunshine, streaking their clothes, their hair, their skin, everywhere. It took them a long time to get clean afterwards, puddling in the bottom of the scratchy tin bath and throwing buckets of water over each other. Exhausting. They stretched themselves out on Asmodus' cushions, waiting for the sun to dry their hair.

"You on holiday today?" Dasha asked.

"Sort of. I told them I was sick." Stéphane shifted about, trying to get comfortable. There was something hard thrusting a corner up through the cushions. She burrowed underneath them and pulled out a book: not an ordinary book, more like a wad of tissue paper two inches thick, massively bound in leather, crumbling into a pinkish rot round the edges. *LETTERS*, the spine informed her. Whose letters? She opened the book with the tips of her fingers, as though it might be infectious. Wharf letters, business dating from the 1890's.

"Is that where it got to?" Dasha ran her hand fondly over the worn cover. One of Asmodus' treasures, grubbed out of a heap of junk at the bottom of the Black Hole. "How's that, you're sick?"

"I'm sick of my office. I wanted to be here instead, that's all."

"You're all right then." Dasha look relieved.

"Of course! Don't I look it? It was only an excuse for a day off. Like the time I came here in the boat, that first day." Stéphane fell silent, caught off balance by the expression in Dasha's eyes, one she hadn't seen often enough yet. Kindness, but troubled.

"Yes, you look fine." Dasha said. "You don't look so pale, like you used to."

"It's good for me here."

The reply was a murmur that Stéphane couldn't catch. "What did you say?" She propped herself up on her elbows and took a careful look at Dasha's face. "Why have you gone quiet?"

"I said, I know. I just wish you could be here whenever you liked, without having to make excuses. It's a shame for you."

Stéphane smiled, a reassuring smile. "That's nothing, I'm used to it, everybody does it. Lies, damned lies, and statistics." Luxuriously, she rolled over and stretched out in a patch of sun, closing her eyes.

"What's that?"

"I can't just remember who said it. A prime minister. The three different kinds of lies."

"Don't tell me that. Who needs it?"

Stéphane opened her eyes and squinted up, shocked. "What's got into you now?"

"Maybe you tell me lies too."

"That's a stupid thing to say. Of course I don't. I don't need to. Most other people I do, even if it's only to save their feelings. But not you."

"I know, I'm stupid. Only don't ever tell me lies – and I'm being very stupid now, really stupid – because I love you, but you, even the bits you don't want me to see."

"Dasha! Where's the Prince? Dasha!"

Nancy's voice penetrated five layers of floorboards.

"I love you too," Stéphane said, thinking that there was more truth in that than in anything she'd ever said before.

"DA - SHA!"

Nancy burst in. "Didn't you —um," she stopped, confused, and made a clumsy retreat backwards, nearly catching her heel on a cat. "Excuse me," she muttered.

"I'll be right down." Dasha smiled at her over Stéphane's shoulder, and unclasped her arms. "You want to come down too, Fantast?"

"No, I don't think so. I'll only be in the way. You go, I'll be happy by myself for a while."

*

When Pink came in an hour later, Stéphane was still sitting by the window, reading the letters.

"Oh, I'm sorry." He smiled at her, in a puzzled way. "I didn't know you were here."

She closed the book and smiled back at him. "Am I sitting on your cushions? I'm the one who should be sorry. I was only trying to keep out of Nancy's way."

"You as well?" He thought that was funny. "We're all trying to do that. Still, we're safe enough here. I think we are, anyway. D'you like those letters? I do." He wandered over, shyly, and sat down opposite her. "They were all so polite to each other, your obedient servant, and things like that. Typewritten, though. Even in 1904."

"Yes, that surprised me too . . . well, at the end here all the letters seem to be about war risks and ships being sunk. It all gets a bit sad."

"We never found any more letters after 1917." Pink brushed some dust off his ankle, and stared into space. "I suppose this place started being a relic then. The people who built it thought that it would last for hundreds of years, didn't they? They must have really believed in themselves."

Stéphane nodded. The confident tissue of words that made up the letters: Commerce. Industry. Profit. The Market. Just words in an old book of letters, as worn out as the wharf they were left in.

"It's not like that anymore, is it?"

"No."

A tourist-boat came past, reminding them of former glories and present dereliction. Pink stared at the backs of his hands. "I was wondering," he hesitated.

"No, go on. Please."

"I was wondering," he tried again, "if you would like to see my studio? Where I paint, and everything," he rushed on, "only if you'd like to, I mean, not if you'd rather   "

"I would like to. I really would." She was glad he'd invited her. She would have been too shy to ask.

Pink fussed over his stepladder, "Are you sure?" and clambered up it through the studio trapdoor. He peered over the edge. "Give

47

me your hand, the ladder's tricky. Careful, don't step on that cracked one."

Stéphane managed to get in, finally, by landing on her knees. Anxiously Pink dusted her off while she reassured him, she hadn't hurt herself, and tried to make sense of his junk-room. Studio?

Gritty ochre dusting on tangles of wood and canvas, buckets of papier-mâché, brushes turning into fossils on the floor, random gobs of paint smeared everywhere, mixed up with crusts and pieces of cheese-rind, bottles, cigarette-papers. Stéphane's eyes fixed on the simplest object, in the centre of the room. A grecian plinth wearing a crown.

"Nancy got me to make some things for Xanadu," Pink explained. "That's the Prince's crown. It's not quite finished yet."

Stéphane picked her way over to the plinth and stood for a while admiring the crown, then walked all round it to wonder at the way it was made: spiky silver and brilliant with crystals. In the centre, hung round with tiny chiming fragments of coloured glass, was a mirror.

She stepped back, not wanting to look at her own reflection.

"You don't think it's too much, do you?" Pink wanted to know. "I couldn't decide whether it ought to be silver or gold, but Nancy said silver, sort of cosmic-looking, she said." He shrugged, nervously.

Stéphane grinned. "I'm sure." She could imagine Nancy saying it.

"But look at this." Pink called her attention away, to a life-size cardboard cut-out propped in the corner. "This is the ogre of Xanadu. His back-view. No-one else has seen him yet. Only you."

She bowed to the compliment, silently giving her respect to Pink's skill. It was the most brutish, deformed view she could ever have imagined, of an ogre's back.

"He's supposed to be asleep," Pink said.

Stéphane raised her eyebrows. How could he be asleep when he was standing up?

"They're like horses, they can go to sleep on their feet. But he's got a front too."

Pink trotted over to lift up the ogre, awkwardly, and began to turn it round to show that it had a face. "Cover your eyes until I've finished turning it over."

"Is it as frightening as that?"

"As dreadful as I could make it. You can look now."

Stéphane breathed in sharply. Its expression was one of terrible, lost sadness. She stared at it without knowing what to say.

"I know." Pink stood the cut-out back in its corner. "Nancy won't like it either. But I'm not going to do another one. She'll manage."

"Why –" Stéphane's question was cut off by the ogre falling flat on its back. Pink sighed and propped it up again. "Only the ghost having fun. Did you say something?"

"Just the obvious. Why so sad?"

"I think I'd look sad if I knew everyone wanted to steal my treasure, and nobody loved me. Wouldn't you?" He laughed, as though he wanted to make sure she wouldn't take offence.

"I suppose I would." Poor creature, prowling round in its void. Nobody loves me, everybody hates me. It suddenly occurred to Stéphane that love meant a great deal to Pink, but she left the subject alone until he had shown her more of his paintings. There, the same undertow, felt but not spoken about, until he came to his latest one. Gabriel's Breastplate, based on the colours and shapes of the wharf: an attempt to express the way he loved the building. Pink struggled to explain it, but his voice mumbled away into an anxious silence.

Stéphane felt sorry for him. "I love the wharf too," she said gently, "but I wouldn't know how to show what I felt about it. In a painting, I mean. Even though I wanted to be an artist once." She stamped on the thought, and threw Pink's burden back to him. "Tell me what you think about love, then."

She wished she hadn't asked. Why had she asked that? If only she could have said something flippant, to bring everything back to the polite conversation level. But he considered her question innocently enough, not seeming to notice her embarrassment. "I would tell you if I could. It's strange about you, I wouldn't mind telling you things I couldn't say to anyone else, except Asmodus perhaps." He stared at his feet for a while. "I don't mean love in the let's make love sense, though that's part of it. I don't know what love is, that's the point, and I'll never know, but everything comes back to it in the end. Just because it can accept everything and outlast everything. I think that's all my life's for, learning about it, even when I tell myself I don't want to know."

He turned away, confused, and started scraping at a blob of paint on the wall. There was nothing else for him to say, and Stéphane turned away too, looking for something to occupy her attention for a while. Just a decent pause, until they could begin talking about something else.

Pink stopped what he was doing, and listened. There was a scratching noise at the trapdoor, like an outsize rat trying to get in. "Open up, my loves! What are you doing in there? My wife and I are coming to get you. Nancy sent us! Thank you." Asmodus swivelled his head round the opening, and hopped up the last few rungs of the ladder, reaching down to help Dasha join him.

"The crown", he panted. "Where is it?"

"But it's not finished yet," Pink wailed.

"Oh, rubbish, it looks fine. Doesn't it, my love? Dasha? If you and Stéphane would stop gazing into each others' eyes for just a second, I'm asking you what you think."

"Yes, it's fine," Dasha said absently. "It's lovely. Thank you." She pulled herself together and took hold of the crown carefully, placing it for a few seconds on Stéphane's head. "Magnificent. Look, I can see myself in it. Asmodus, look."

"Vain, horrible creature." Asmodus was half-way down the ladder again. "Come on, they're all waiting for you."

"All right, just a minute." Dasha stood thinking, because she'd noticed how Stéphane and Pink looked, lost, as though they didn't know what to do next. "Can you come down?" she asked, "and give us a hand? Please, I *need* you. You want me to end up wringing Nancy's neck, or what?"

Stéphane and Pink looked at each other, and then followed her down, laughing. They knew exactly what she meant.

*

After a few visits to the wharf, Stéphane had grown skilful at wading through the cats without treading on them. The secret was not to take your feet off the floor. Once outside the door, she could keep the cats at bay by swinging one leg to and fro, just low enough to thump them in the whiskers if they tried an all-out attack.

Pink opened the door, hiding a tin of dogfood behind his back. "Hello," he said. "What a nice surprise, we never expect you so early. Come and sit by the window. Dasha's not here at the moment, she's gone out. But she won't be long."

Asmodus greeted Stéphane with more decorum, placing her in the middle of his best cushions – "I myself will sit on this festering heap over here" – and they all sat down to smile at each other.

"I'm not disturbing you, am I?" Stéphane asked.

"Of course not, no, not at all." Asmodus took up his notebook, expansively. "I was just polishing my pamphlet." He looked at Pink. "Shall I tell her about it?"

He was so tempted to expound his theory to a new audience that he threw caution to the winds. "Why not? Stéphane, I think of you as one of us now. Would you like to hear about my pamphlet?"

"Very much."

He explained that it was a brilliant attack on outmoded duality-concepts: peace and war, freedom and equality, men and women, all that sort of worn-out rubbish. It was an utter waste of time, creating opposites and then trying to reconcile them. You had to transcend them, then they wouldn't exist. "Do you see? So my pamphlet tells you how."

Stéphane read through it. She only took four minutes, because it was only five pages long.

"Well?" Asmodus asked, leaning forward.

"It's very good. I like this bit about the sublime reality-condition of everlastingness."

"Do I detect a 'but' in your voice?"

"But," Stéphane agreed doubtfully, "there isn't very much of it, is there?"

Asmodus drew himself up with dignity. "What," he queried, "has that got to do with it? I am not going to write multi-million page epics. I've got television to contend with. These days, people like something they can read in four minutes. It was all right for people to sit around all day reading in Tolstoy's time. The end of the world was still a hundred years away."

"I tried reading *Lottie in Weimar*, once," offered Pink, by way of trying to soothe the atmosphere.

"That's not Tolstoy. What about it?"

"I don't know . . . after I'd got to page 397 and they'd only had two conversations, I didn't bother with it anymore."

"See what I mean?" Asmodus lifted his finger triumphantly. "That exactly proves my point. Exactly."

Pink wandered off, dispirited, to buy a pint of milk and a few eggs.

Asmodus rearranged his cushions. "So much for our resident intellectual. I'd never have thought he'd read anything, even comics, let alone *Lotte in Weimar*. He likes to keep our togetherness fresh with little surprises."

"Don't be hard on him."

"Why not?"

"He's very beautiful, the way he paints and sees things."

"He's been talking to you about love being the centre of the universe."

"Yes, that's right." Stéphane sounded surprised. "It made me think."

"What would you think if I said that the universe trundles on regardless, and the only person Pink's ideas work for is Pink?"

Stéphane hesitated. "I don't know."

"Well then, you can't have thought about it much."

"No, I suppose not," Stéphane said humbly, hoping that due deference would stop Asmodus attacking her any more. But Asmodus was no gentleman.

"What *do* you think about?" he pursued, thrusting his nose forward.

"Oh, my work, and friends, and things like that."

"No, I mean important things."

"Like what?"

"Well, for instance, what makes you happy?"

Stéphane made a gesture as though she were throwing feathers in the air. "Being here makes me happy," she said lightly, hating herself for feeling foolish.

"Has anyone else ever asked you what makes you happy?" Asmodus asked, more kindly.

"I can't remember . . . yes, a teacher asked us once, at school. When it was sunny we'd sit on the lawn sometimes. I forget why she asked it." Stéphane's voice faded, uncertainly.

"No, go on. What did you say?"

"I said being happy was when you didn't want anything."

"I don't think you can have been a very nice child."

"It seemed clever at the time. Just a clever answer to get me a pat on the head. I probably read it in a book. It didn't seem a very useful thing to worry about. Knowing what made me happy wasn't going to help me pass exams, I remember thinking, none of the things the other girls said would make me happy, like lots of money or lots of babies, things like that. But I couldn't see myself ever getting to a state where I wouldn't want anything, so I didn't waste my time worrying about it any more."

It sounded all wrong. Asmodus would tear her to pieces for saying such futile things. She lifted her hand, ready to fend off the claws.

But Asmodus only smiled. "I would suggest," he pontificated, "that you give the subject some thought, because if you don't know what makes you happy I don't see how you can keep Dasha happy either."

Stéphane laughed, unsure of herself. "This is like being at school."

"I don't think you know what schools are for. Schools are for putting people to sleep. No school would ever encourage you to do the things I say." Asmodus took up his notebook again, muttering the occasional word to himself in a tone of delighted admiration.

Stéphane leaned back and crossed her legs, irritated at herself for being so feeble: losing control of the conversation and letting Asmodus push her into wretched corners. It wasn't a feeling she was used to, and she resented it. She set her teeth in a determined line, but he came back at her again before she could think of anything suitably brilliant or crushing to say to him.

"Does your job make you happy?"

She groaned. "Let's drop it, shall we, all this happy talk?"

"Certainly, if you just answer my question."

"All right then, no," she snapped. "I'd give it up if I could."

"Why can't you? I should give it up anyway. Jobs aren't made for people like us, they only suit people who think they're men and women."

"What?" She stared at him, with her mouth slightly open.

He coiled himself up and began to fiddle with his leg-warmers, pulling off little bobbles of matted wool and placing them, with exaggerated care, in a fluffy heap. "Or more precisely," he said, "for people who think they're women. By the time women can do all the work and run things, all the men will have decided it's no fun anymore and they'll go off to do something like cultivating their souls, you know, something more *manly,* that only men can do, and leave mundane things, like jobs, to the opposite sex, as I believe they call it. Not," he added, "that there's anything right or wrong about that, of course, it's just the way dualism works. Keeping the differences alive."

She closed her eyes, reeling at the prospect of such lunatic unreality, taking refuge in sarcasm while she put her thoughts back together.

"Will there be time for all that before the end of the world?"

"There is no world," he replied distantly, and lapsed into a profound contemplation of his knees.

She had suspected it; she had, ever since she met him. He was insane. Terrifying thought. She closed her eyes again, squeezing them tight this time, and prayed for deliverance, for Dasha to walk in and rescue her.

"Tell me more about yourself." Asmodus' voice was gentle. He didn't really understand why he'd frightened her, but he hadn't meant to. "Do you like music? Poetry? I like music."

Weren't you supposed to humour madmen? "I used to like music, a lot," Stéphane said uneasily, feeling an echo of something sad, that had to do with flowers in a forest. She remembered the music she'd enjoyed, when she was a student; she could listen to it for hours, turned up so loud it made her ears crackle. It made her feel sensitive. And profound. Loving. "But it never has the same effect when I play it now. It embarrasses me, almost."

She felt so tired, suddenly, that she wanted to cry.

"Of course, my love! It's not appropriate any more. But don't be sad about it. Think of discovering all those new wonders waiting for you," he waved his hand, casually, "wherever you go to next. Dasha will help you find them, if you don't let her leave."

"Leaving?" The only thing Stéphane understood was that he said Dasha was going to go away. Her eyelids began to sting. "Is she?"

"Well, yes, I suppose we'll all be going away sometime, and her sooner than the rest of us. But she'll stay if you want her to. She'll do anything, you know, if you ask."

Stéphane didn't reply.

Asmodus turned away to stare out of the window. "Anything," he murmured, wonderng if even Dasha could wake a sleeping beauty who had probably never, once, thought an idea that hadn't been told her by someone else.

Hollow-eyed, his reflection stared back at him. And behind that, he saw Dasha leaning against the doorway, quite still. Strange, that neither he nor Stéphane had noticed Dasha come in.

There was no peace in the wharf these days. You couldn't even have a thoughtful talk without other people intruding, coming up on you like thieves in the night. If it wasn't Pink or Nancy, it was Dasha.

"Now you see me, now you don't," she said, moving forward to stand behind Stéphane. "Does Asmodus need to tell you what I'll do if you ask me?" She reached down to touch Stéphane's fingers. "Go away, Asmodus. You should never make people cry."

"It wasn't his fault, he didn't make me cry," Stéphane pleaded. "Sometimes I do, and I don't even know why. See, I can have a perfectly rational conversation with tears pouring down my face."

Oh, my sad love, Dasha thought, what a temptation it is, kissing tears away. But you don't want that, do you? It'll only make you cry even more. A rational conversation? All right.

She smiled, and brought Asmodus' shopping bag in from the doorway where she'd dropped it. "It's Hallowe'en tomorrow. Did anyone tell you what we're going to do?"

Stéphane tried hard to be interested.

"We're going to have a birthday party." Dasha continued, "for the wharf ghost. Asmodus wants to make a cake, and Pink's going to do the decorations. Look, I've been buying things for it."

Boxes of candles and stars, a tin of florescent paint, a bottle of gin, a plastic flute and a toy drum.

"What are you going to do with it all?"

"The gin, you can guess. The rest, wait and see."

"Does the ghost know it's his birthday party?"

"For sure."

"And if he doesn't want to come?"

"He'll come. Asmodus' cakes are special."

"Asmodus was telling me about his pamphlet," Stéphane said.

"Beyond-duality-into-everlastingness?"

"I think so."

"You're honoured." Dasha looked away, as though she wanted to laugh. "Even I'm not supposed to have seen that one yet. Though I don't know who else is going to read it, apart from you and me and Pink. Maybe Nancy." She lay back on her elbows and crossed her feet. "It's a shame for him, he went on for a whole afternoon last year, telling me how nobody reads his pamphlets. He spends all that time picking over every word, and then copying them."

Last year Asmodus found an ancient spirit duplicator outside a youth-club, and tottered home with it perched on his pram, and worshipped it for weeks. But he couldn't make it work, and then he got mad because Pink trod some blobs of ink into the cushions. Bye bye duplicator. "And after all that he even gives them away, but still nobody wants to read them."

Stéphane managed a half-smile. "If he wants everyone to read them, he ought to stick a huge price on them and say they're only for the chosen few."

"You know, I told him that once, not long after I met him."

"And?"

"He sat up very straight, you know like he does, and he said, 'If it costs money, it ain't the truth.' But really, if you have to read it in a pamphlet, I guess it's not the truth either. Could be one reason people don't want to read what he writes."

"He said I ought to give up my job."

"All right, Fantast. All right." Dasha put her arm round Stéphane's waist and drew her back against the wall. "I know when you're not listening to me. There, that more comfortable for you? Go on then, tell me what else he said, the old witch."

"Oh, I can't remember, he asked if I was happy, and then he said a lot of stuff about jobs only being for men and women, I don't know."

Dasha nodded. That, she could imagine; she'd heard it all before. But she wanted to know what Stéphane thought, even if it meant sitting up all night, trying to keep awake listening in the dragged-out silences.

"In a way, I know what he means," Stéphane admitted. "I've felt it for a long time, I suppose, but I never wanted to do any thinking about it. Well, really, I always thought that anything doubtful, that I wasn't sure about, destructive, anything like that would just go away, if I worked harder at whatever I was doing. Until I came here," she added, miserably.

Dasha laughed, so suddenly and joyously that Stéphane crumbled into a bewildered silence.

"I'm sorry," Dasha said, "but you sounded just like my mother, really, you did. She thought that anything that wasn't *nice* would disappear if she switched on the television. I couldn't even talk to her in the end, she just had it on the whole time. Full blast. Oh, you. If you're going to take your job so seriously, and get so down about it, maybe you better had give it up." She stretched her voice out, thinning it a little with affected weariness. "Dont you know, my love, that there are only five jobs, all equally tiresome and pointless? They're only a way of filling in time until the clock stops."

A sound, mid-way between a cough and a snigger, muffled itself against Dasha's shoulder.

"Right." Dasha followed it up, swiftly. "So what have you been thinking, that isn't nice?"

Stéphane sat up and began to trace patterns with her fingernails, round the burn-marks on a velvet cushion. "When I told my father I wanted to be an artist," she brought out at last, "he said I'd never be more than a tenth-rate one, and I had brains enough to do something more useful." She shrugged. "I believed him, that's all. I got used to it. After a while I even began to pat myself on the head for choosing such a good job, and not wasting my time being a useless artist. Me! How did I get to be where I am?" She broke off, curiously, as though she couldn't remember much about the last ten years. "All I know is now, I spend most of my time working and it's very interesting and they give me lots of money, and if I had a wife and kids to do it for, if it all fitted into something else, it'd probably make sense. But it doesn't, and it scares me —" she swallowed. "It frightens me when I think I haven't got any sort of life outside it." Lifting up her hands, and then letting them drop in frustration, she came to the nastiest thought of all. "I know it's my own fault I don't know what I want; it's easier to make do with what other people tell you to want. I don't even know if there's anything else I can do."

"How about stopping what you're doing, if you know you don't want to do it anymore." Dasha was lying on the floor now, with her hands behind her head, staring up at a crack that ran inwards from the window. It was a new crack, that hadn't been there before. Or she'd never noticed it. She heard Stéphane say:

"I can't get up and leave, just like that. It's not possible. I'm in the middle of something – that I can't stop working on." The usual hesitation, always when she veered away from what she was doing. "It's not the right time."

Dasha sighed. "All right, so it's impossible. Whatever you want to do, it never is the right time to do it." She sat up abruptly, and arranged herself back against the wall. "You wait for the right time to do anything, you'll wait till you're dead, so you don't have to worry about what if it goes wrong."

"What sort of advice is that? Wait till you're dead, that's no help."

"You expect me to take over from all the other people who told you what to do? I'm not that clever. If you want my advice, and you won't like it, if you want my advice, just do like Nancy and her videos. If you want to do something different with your life, just do it and see what happens. You don't have to know what it's about before you start. You'll find things out as you go along, and they'll be your things, not anyone else's." She stopped suddenly, and rested her chin on her hands, struck by an awareness of something she wanted herself, with complete certainty. "Close you eyes now, imagine a roundabout horse for me. One wish." If she could have given away all the wishes of her life except one, this would be it.

Stéphane closed her eyes.

I wish, Dasha thought, that you'll want me there with you, whatever it is you do.

"Finished?" Stéphane relaxed and settled her head against Dasha's chest. "Have you stopped going on at me now? Can I ask you something?"

"Mm."

"Is it true, what Asmodus said about you going away soon?"

"He said we'll all be going away."

"But you first?"

"Me first, and then you. Or the other way round. Or both of us together. It depends on you. Anything you ask, he said. That's true too."

"I'm asking you. Don't go. Not yet."

"I don't want to go. Not yet."

*

Pink had woken up early enough, for once, to join in the morning coffee ritual. He stood in the doorway, listening to Asmodus clattering pans and then, for a moment, felt a sharp delight that Dasha and Stéphane were there, deep in conversation by the window. They reminded him of Klingsor's princesses, who passed their days arguing over poetry and beauty.

"Have you only just got up?" Asmodus looked round, beakily. "Isn't today your day for signing on?"

Pink looked stricken. It was. He'd forgotten again. He couldn't be late this time. He was late last time. Mr. Sharpe would be furious.

"You won't be late," Stéphane said. "I'll give you a lift."

Asmodus cackled. "What will Mr Sharpe say if he looks out of his window and sees Pink arriving in a BMW? He'll cut you off without a penny, angel."

"Do you think so?" Pink flinched at the unthinkable.

Stéphane shook her head, trying to reassure him without contradicting Asmodus. She would drop Pink where Mr. Sharpe couldn't see. It was time to go, anyway.

For part of the way she drove in silence, following Pink's directions almost absent-mindedly. Left at the end of the road, right at the roundabout. Then she said, without looking at him:

"Where would you live, if you didn't have the wharf?"

The cold anxiety in her voice was startling, even more than the question. Pink hesitated, not knowing how to hold out his hand over the no-man's land that divided her cares from his.

"I don't know, I never worry about it. I didn't have anywhere before, till Asmodus found me. By the river. Not far from here even, though he didn't live in the wharf then. I suppose we'd go back to the river, sail away and see where the boat ended up. Can you turn left at the lights, just drop me anywhere along that street."

She pulled over, and sat for a few seconds with her chin resting on the wheel, amused in spite of herself at the thought of Pink and Amodus sailing away in Trio. The owl and the pussycat. How far would they get? It was impossible; it would soon be winter. "Well," she said. "don't worry about it. See you this evening."

If there had been more time, Pink would have drifted away up the street, wondering what Stéphane meant he shouldn't worry about. But there was no time for that. He trotted in through Door B and presented himself.

"Mr Knight?" The girl behind the counter produced a slip of paper from some secret shelf, and handed it to him. "You've got to sign this as well. You're down to see Mr Sharpe today," she added anxiously.

The mention of Mr Sharpe created a horrible feeling in Pink's stomach. He took the paper and began the long creep down the corridor to Room 69, composing himself into the trance-like state of feeble-mindedness which was the only way to be during encounters with Mr Sharpe.

"Ah, Philip. Do come in. Sit down."

It was clear that Mr Sharpe was going to be especially tiresome this morning. Philip, he had said. The only people who ever referred to Pink as Philip were his mother (when he had done something wrong) and Mr Sharpe, generally as a cheerful touch slipped in between the words "come now," and "be reasonable."

"Hello, Mr Sharpe," said Pink humbly, sitting down on the edge of a green plastic chair.

Mr Sharpe was not skilled in the pitter-patter of small talk, but preferred to get straight to the point, not beat about the bush with hard cases like the one drooping in front of him.

"Well, no change in your situation since last time, I see."

"No, Mr Sharpe."

"Been for any interviews?"

"No, I don't think so."

There was a silence, while Mr Sharpe cast around for something constructive to say.

"Well then, Philip, what do you think you would most like to do if you could choose? Though of course," he added hurriedly, "we can't all choose exactly what we would like."

Pink pretended to give the question profound consideration.

"I think I would like to spend my time painting beautiful pictures," he said at last.

Mr Sharpe sneered. "Oh, we'd all like to sit at home and paint! Well then, let me put it another way. Just supposing there were no Social Security, what would you do then?"

Pink let his eyes wander unfocussed around the room. "I think I'd commit suicide," he said vaguely.

Mr Sharpe coughed. "We're not being very positive today, are we? Believe it or not, I really am trying to help you. You could get a job if you wanted to. There are thousands of jobs you could do. But you have to help me to help you. Otherwise I shall have no alternative but to refer you to my superiors in Room 103 A."

Room 103 A! Oh no, please, Mr Sharpe, not Room 103 A! Isn't that the room next to the Jobshop?

"I can see that doesn't appeal to you. Very well, Philip, I'm going to give you one last chance. I'm not an unreasonable man, I think you'll agree? I cannot think, I would be extremely grieved to think, that you don't actually want to do a proper job, will you pay attention please, and make a contribution to society."

Pink bowed his head.

"No," continued Mr Sharpe with a touch of compassion. "I should prefer to believe that you would welcome a chance to make your contribution. It so happens that I can offer you two chances, here and now. Take them. Choose one."

Pink took the cards and mouthed over the job descriptions to himself.

One was a job as a toilet attendant in a hostel for trainee bank managers. How appropriate he thought. The other job was as teaboy messenger in a large firm of City architects.

Pink handed the cards back.

"I can't really decide, Mr Sharpe. Perhaps I'll try the teaboy one first."

*

"Are you still here?" Martin came into the front room, where Stéphane had been reading by the fire. It looked as though she had nearly finished the book: it lay open in her lap while she stared into the flames, the last few pages drifting idly in the heat.

He settled himself down in his armchair, the larger one, Mr Armchair, as Stéphane called it, and stretched out, resting his feet on the fire-surround.

"You seem to be reading a lot lately," he remarked.

"Mm."

He watched her out of the corner of his eye. And she seemed to want to be by herself a lot lately, too. What was the use, going on like this: there had to be a limit to anyone's patience, even his. A piece of damp timber shifted in the grate, and spat, and a grimy spider scuttled out across the hearth, away from the light.

"What are you reading?" Martin asked, trying to keep back the irritation spiking in his voice. "Stop ignoring me. I'm here. Talk to me."

"I'm sorry." Letting the book drop down the side of her chair, she looked round at him. "I've let the fire get too low. I'll cheer it up for us." He watched her pick up the old sword from its place by the grate, and poke the cinders with it, roughly, so that a rush of sparks flew up crackling. Then she threw in another log and crouched back against the wall, watching it take.

"You still haven't told me what you were reading."

"Oh, yes. Nothing really. A book about the history of the old wharves. I got it out of the library." She picked up a long splinter and began doodling patterns in the ash. "What they were like in the nineteenth century."

"Whatever for?" His eyes narrowed. "I can't see how that's any help when your job's designing something new. Just finding out more about a place that's going to be demolished, what's the point?"

A quick look. "It's the site that matters. You said so yourself. I'm trying to work out something that feels right, for the site." Stéphane dropped her eyes and went back to her doodling.

"Oh, I don't understand you. At all. Remember the first day we spent here? In this room, here, when you talked all the time about the ideas you had for the project?"

No, it wasn't like that, she wanted to remind him. Most of the ideas were yours.

"You had so many ideas, you weren't even going to bother taking another look at the wharf. Not bother, that's what you said. And then the next thing I heard, you'd gone round there in that boat. Didn't you? Why?"

"Maybe I wish I never had bothered." She threw the splinter back in the fire and slumped down in Mrs Armchair, listlessly. "I'm sorry."

"I wish you wouldn't keep saying you're sorry. I'm sorry too. Look, we shouldn't be talking like this. We shouldn't." He reached out for her hand, giving it a little shake. "Let me help you, that's all I want to do. Tell me what the matter is, then I can do something about it. What's wrong with you? Is it the wharf?"

"Partly." No use denying it. "I think it began with that." Perhaps it did begin there, with those hideous, soulless designs. "What did you really think, when you were looking over my drawings?"

He hedged. "That's hard, asking me what I think of something that's only half-finished." But that wasn't the answer she wanted. "I think they're fine," he said firmly. "I like them."

"I don't." She said it mechanically, as though she'd repeated the words so many times they hardly meant anything now. I don't like the designs I've done. "I've even gone back and looked at the other buildings I've worked on." Thinking that they had been more inspired than the wharf project. They weren't. "They were just the same." The same pattern-book tricks, the same artists' impressions of people living like angels, liberated by all that airy light and comfort; abstract masses in free flow, dissolving into the ungrateful reality of concrete footsteps, hurried and menacing, and sideways glances at strangers on the other side of a glass wall. "My designs don't work, that's all. The wharf project isn't going to work."

"My poor Stéphane, can't you choose some other time to start losing confidence in yourself?" Martin laughed, uncertainly, and squatted down beside her, as though he were about to address a child at what he imagined was its own level. "Is that really all it is? I should have guessed, it meant so much to you and you wanted to do so well, you've frightened yourself into a block about it. Don't be silly." He gave her hands another shake. "Shall I tell you what's going to happen now? You're going to carry on with your plans just as you've started them, because there's absolutely nothing wrong with them. Would I say I liked them, otherwise? Luckily for us. There wouldn't be any time to do them over. And we don't need to." If he had any doubts, he knew it was the wrong time to show them. Certainty was all it needed, confidence enough to carry both of them along. He thought of all the money he'd put into the project, and felt sticky.

"How much time have I got to finish?" she asked.

"As much time as I gave you before. Isn't that enough?" He stood up and added, more quietly, "Stéphane, I *want* that building to start going up before next spring, and no delays. Remember that, and you won't have any time to worry about it. You'll see I'm right. When we watch them build it, we'll be laughing about what you said this afternoon. So that's the wharf problem solved." He sighed, happily, and looked down at her. "Give me a smile now. Can't you do that? Don't tell me there's anything else wrong."

No, I won't tell you. I wouldn't know how to. She smiled up at him, and then looked away. It's not just the wharf, Martin. It's everything. The wharf, us, my work, everything. All kinds of things I've been pushing to the back of my mind for years. They're all coming out now, and I can't push them back anymore.

He was still looking down at her, concerned that she seemed to tired, and he told her so as gently as he could.

He was right, she was tired. "Maybe," she said, "I just need to go away by myself for a little while, take time off to think about a few things properly."

He nodded, thinking that she'd said it too casually, without much sincerity. Trying not to hurt his feelings? "It it me you want to get away from?" he asked, sharply.

"I don't know." The reply was equally bitter.

Martin turned his back and rested his arms on the mantelpiece, asking himself how old she was: he never could remember. Younger than him, that was all. It might be about her age that women had to decide whether they wanted children, now or never. Perhaps that was the trouble. "If you," he started, and then thought better of it. He couldn't talk to her about that. No, she was still much too young to be worried about lost chances.

"What were you going to say?"

"It doesn't matter. Nothing important. Look, you don't have to go away. I'll go away. I'm going away for two weeks tomorrow, that's it, and I'll leave my phone numbers at the office, if you need to talk to me. But you don't have to. Then when I come back, you'll have thought about things and you can tell me what you want. I'm not going to change, I still know what I want. I want you. I need to have you around," and he laughed, "because I can't talk to anyone else the way I can talk to you. So let's not spoil the rest of today being gloomy now. Come on out. Let's see how many pubs we can get through in one evening."

*

Dead leaves had rained all over the pavements: there was no wind to move them and nobody had come to sweep them away. Only Pink's feet stirred a few of them as he scuffled towards the unknown. Day number one in the life of a teaboy: his days were numbered.

He wasn't awake yet; his eyes ached with the sparkling pavements and the hard flat sky, the cruel fresh air, diamond-blue. It was always the same when they forced him to do jobs. Getting up too early, arriving half-asleep, and only feeling more and more tired as the day wore on.

He found the building and walked in without curiosity, stared blankly at the receptionist when she asked if he had an appointment. He didn't know, but he had this letter in his pocket . . . it said he was to ask for E.M. Battley (Mrs), Office Supervisor.

Mrs Battley was a very busy lady, so she wasn't going to waste time introducing Pink to everybody. She was far too busy for that. Briskly, she launched him into the flood-tide of his duties.

"You must look after the letters, and take them to the post. That's twice a day. At twelve o'clock and at four-thirty sharp. Sometimes letters and packages have to be delivered by hand. You do that. You make the tea, and you bring it round to the office staff at eleven and three. The partners have their own coffee machines but some of them like a cup of tea in the afternoon. The partners are on the seventh floor. You must never, under any circumstances, go up there in the mornings. And you must always knock before you go in."

Pink gripped his hands behind his back, wrestling with his desire to yawn in the face of so much stultifying organisation. Eleven, tea; twelve, letters; three, tea; four-thirty, letters. Every day. Knock humbly on the doors of the gods. Five-thirty, atishoo atishoo, all go home. He had made a dreadful mistake. The trainee bank-managers and their toilets would have been more fun.

But Mrs Battley had started on her favourite subject: the partners. She knew them well, of course. It was her responsibility to look after them all, though sometimes, she couldn't resist adding, they took one for granted. The most important person was Mr Harkness, the senior partner. He was so awesomely important that hardly anyone ever saw him. Mr Harkness's secretary made Lapsang Suchong tea for him in her own office, so Pink would probably never see him at all . . . .

Her voice droned on. Mr Barrington, who was fussy, Mr. Cox, Mr Howard, Mr Drake. Pink pulled himself together and paid attention. Mr Drake was the most talented of them all, and so young to be a partner. But not at all conceited, always ready to joke and treat one almost as an equal. Oh, and there was one other partner, Miss LeNormant. She kept herself to herself, and didn't often want tea. Miss LeNormant was very involved in a big project. Mrs Battley frowned, implying that she would have thought Mr Drake should have the big project.

"LeNormant?" Pink's eyes opened wide. "Is she called Stéphane? Stéphane LeNormant?"

Mrs Battley stared at him with dislike. "I believe so," she said suspiciously. "But in this office it's Miss LeNormant to you."

And she dismissed him to the post-room.

Pink spent the morning in a delighted haze, gloating in secret over his luck. None of it mattered; not Mrs Battley's nagging, nor the clown who flapped his wrists and called Pink sweetie, nor the typists who tittered. Pink only smiled vaguely, absorbed in his imagination of the wonderful scene set for three o'clock, when he took Stéphane her tea. Stéphane's amazement, Pink's throwing himself on her mercy, his lips quivering, begging her to help him escape. Then she would smile, warmly and graciously like she always did, and sack him on the spot. It was too good to be true.

"Have you taken the partners their tea yet?"

"No, Mrs Battley, I was just going."

In the bland stillness of the seventh floor his trolley made a trundling sound, and kept sinking into the carpet. Pink abandoned it by the lift and tiptoed up and down, looking for Stéphane's door.

S. J-L. LeNormant. J-L? Pink held his breath and knocked.

There was no answer. He knocked again, and again no answer. Then he leaned his head against the door, his nose stinging. Oh, Stéphane, why did you have to be out this afternoon?

Somewhere a phone rang, a typewriter clacked. Pink crept back to his trolley and looked around dully, trying to decide what to do next. The first door was A. Drake. All right then, Mr Drake.

Mr Drake was sitting with his feet on the desk, glancing over the International Opportunities page. He looked bored enough to amuse himself with any visitor, even this one.

"Hello," he said, "so you must be Charlie's replacement. Pleased to meet you. I'm Adam Drake, the one who likes gin in his tea."

Pink smiled dutifully.

"Are you settling in alright? D'you have far to come?"

"No thank you, I only live just the other side of the river."

"On the council estate?" Adam condescended.

"No, in Quadrant Street."

"Really." Adam reached forward for his cup of tea, wondering why all these little fairies were such compulsive liars. "I know Quadrant Street," he said idly, "but I didn't think there were any flats there. Only a few warehouses and an old wharf."

"Yes, I live in the wharf."

"What did you say?" Adam put his cup down so sharply that half the tea slopped into the saucer. Pink took a step back and stood looking pathetic, like a rabbit held up by its ears.

"I live in the wharf," he mumbled.

"Gabriel's Wharf?"

"Yes."

Adam smiled thoughtfully, and settled back in his chair. "I am sorry," he said, "I didn't mean to snap at you. So you live in a wharf, do you? How unusual. Tell me, do you know

Martin Geering?"

"No, I don't think so."

"Or Stéphane LeNormant?"

It was an innocent question. Adam sounded as though he really wanted to know. Pink had a feeling, a sick feeling like the one Mr Sharpe gave him. Mr Drake had sly obtuse eyes, like Mr Sharpe.

"No, I don't know her," Pink said instinctively, bending down over his trolley, trying to look natural. Why say he didn't know her? Why feel like flinging himself out of the window? Usual consequences of having done something wrong. Had he? Mr Sharpe, Mr Drake, Mrs Battley, They were all mad. How did Stéphane cope with people like that?

He tinkled a tea-cup to show he didn't care. But Adam was busy on the telephone. His first call didn't reply. He tried someone else. "Sue, where's Stéphane?"

In with Mr Harkness, was the answer. Adam pulled at his moustache. "Just ask her to come and see me when she's free, will you? All right."

He turned back to Pink. "Are you going to stand there all afternoon. I'll send down for you if I want you."

Pink blundered out, desperately trying to force his trolley over the sucking tufts of the carpet. He put his head down and shoved. The trolley lurched into the corridor, nearly running someone down.

"Watch where you're going." Stéphane said.

Pink looked up dumbly. Her face was very white, but if she felt any surprise, she didn't show it. She only stared at him for a moment, and said "Bring me some tea," as she passed on.

*

When a disaster hit her, Stéphane's mind leaped over useless thoughts like why, and how, and recriminations. They could all come later. She concentrated her energies on "what". What had Pink been saying to Adam?

"I didn't say I knew you," he told her breathlessly. "I didn't say that."

Stéphane relaxed.

"But I told him I lived at the wharf."

She passed her hand over her eyes.

In his fright, all Pink could do was cling to his first hope in coming up to the seventh floor. "Will you sack me?" he wailed.

"What?" She seemed to be miles away. "No, of course not. You haven't done anything to be sacked."

"But you don't understand . . . I want to be sacked."

She didn't have to waste time understanding about it.

"Well, in that case, just don't come in tomorrow. I'll make up something for Mrs Battley. Look —" she twisted her cigarette round and round in the ashtray with a careful intensity, as though she were considering setting fire to her desk with it. "Will you do me a favour?"

Pink met her eyes and nodded eagerly.

"We can talk about all this tomorrow," she went on. "No-one's going to be in any fit state tonight."

He agreed: tonight, they all had the World Première of Xanadu to think about. He wouldn't tell anyone about anything, if she didn't want him to. Was she all right?

Even her eyes seemed to have gone a few shades paler.

"Yes, I'm fine," she said, off-handedly, and crushed out her cigarette.

"Shall I go now then?"

"If you don't mind."

Stéphane wondered at herself for not feeling anything; neither fear, nor curiosity, nor any sadness finally, for the way the wharf was going to end. She had lived with the thought for too long.

She moved over to the window and let the view trace itself into her memory. Every shading colour in the rooftops, every shape of each building; she was part of them all, in a moment where nothing changed or ever would change. Down in the street, cars and people moved, but without a sound; she wasn't even aware of them, because they were part of her too. They had no future and no history, existing in the moment, outside time and the world.

Another lost moment. The life and streets and buildings were only the backdrop she had always seen before, and she wanted to scream with loneliness at remembering where she was. Still in her own wretched office, with some business to finish, and she struggled to convince herself that it mattered.

"Did you recognise that – that creature, that just went out?"

Adam was standing in the doorway. He hadn't even bothered to knock.

Stéphane turned round. "I suppose he has a name," she remarked coldly. "Why? Did he say he knew me?"

"He *says* he lives in Gabriel's Wharf."

"Really." She drew in her breath, hesitating, and then nodded. "Well, that's right. He lives in the wharf with a friend of his."

Adam pushed a chair aside, dramatically. Not dramatically enough. He wished he could try the movement over again. However. "You don't mean to tell me you actually knew there were people living there? And you never told anyone? It's not possible! Don't you realise the consequences of that?" A grand gesture, wasted. "Stéphane, are you listening? Tell me it's not true."

She lit another cigarette, and turned back to the window.

"I don't know how you can take it all so calmly," he muttered. She was infuriating. She must know something else. She must be hiding something he ought to know, just so she could enjoy watching him look foolish.

"Don't you realise what you've done?" he repeated, more cautiously.

Still she ignored him.

"Professional misconduct?" he pleaded timidly.

She laughed. "Gross professional misconduct. To the guillotine! Bring your own knitting." Her lips were cracked and dusty, feverish. "No, I mean it." She risked another joke. "Will you miss me?"

He made one last effort to grasp it. "But what reason could you possibly have?"

There was no point in trying to explain: she said the first thing that came into her mind. "I didn't want it to be knocked down. I was trying to hold back the demolition."

He shook his head. "You're not making much sense, are you? D'you know who you sound like? King Canute, that's who."

He reached out and took her hand, smoothing the fingers one by one. "Are you going to resign?"

"That's what I've been wanting to do for days. Weeks."

"My dear, sit down. You look terrible."

"Thank you."

Carefully, they studied the wharf in each others' eyes. He was going to take it away from her, thinking she never had any right to it, even in the beginning; she didn't have the will to destroy it because she knew she couldn't build anything better in its place. And he saw that she loved it, but he couldn't understand why. Maybe the people who lived there thought it was beautiful, but she had made a mess of her life by listening to them.

"These squatters," he said at last. "What are we going to do about them?"

"Nothing."

"What do you mean, nothing? Harkness doesn't know about them, does he?"

"Of course not."

"I'd love to be there when he finds out." Adam sniggered. Squatters would be just the thing to wake the stupid old woman up and send him into one of his rages.

"He's not going to find out."

"Oh? What about Martin, then?"

"Martin," she said patiently, "has gone away. By the time he gets back, I promise you the wharf will be empty."

"You sound very sure of yourself."

"Leave it alone, Adam. I only told you about them because I thought you'd help me."

He laughed, and said that if she hadn't told him, he would have rushed down there, this very evening, to find out what was going on. He was glad she'd saved him the trouble.

He would have been the most unwelcome guest ever to appear at a world première. Stéphane grinned in spite of herself. What would Nancy and her performers have done to a real philistine like Adam? She didn't dwell on the thought. It was too horrible.

"I was going to ask them to leave in any case," she said mildly. "Tomorrow. By the weekend they'll have gone. Let them go quietly. It can't make any difference to you."

"And if they don't go?"

"You'll turn them out anyway, when you take over."

Adam's eyes glinted. "Who says I'm going to take over? It's not for you to say, is it?"

She shrugged.

Adam picked at his nails, thinking. There was an easy way to make sure of getting the wharf. Tell Martin the glad tidings himself. Poor old Martin, poor little Stéphane. He yawned. "All right, have it your own way. I'll leave it alone till the weekend."

*

The World Première of Xanadu. Asmodus had never attended a world première before, and he was beginning to wish that this one had been held somewhere else than his wharf. But he made the best of it and hung around the edges, smiling benignly and acknowledging the greetings of Nancy's thespians.

"Darling! What are you doing here?" Sabrina Slink waved flaky nail varnish in his face. Asmodus stared back, icily. "You know perfectly well I live here," he said with dignity. "I told you when I came to see your last show."

In the day-time, Sabrina did duty as a waiter called Simon. Asmodus sometimes came across her in Earls Court, and usually ended up buying tickets for her shows. The last one had played to a community centre full of bemused immigrants who threw snooker balls at her: Sabrina recalled the event with delight. "Of course, darling . . . Is that Izzie I can see over there? Izebel dearest, I love your new parrot."

Izebel tossed her head – "Haven't you ever seen hair this colour before? you stupid queen" – and turned her back on them.

"Well." Sabrina scanned the tables for a bottle of something strong. "Such a good party. I *am* enjoying myself, aren't you? See you later."

Asmodus sank down, resting his back against a wall, reminding himself severely that all people should be enjoyed for what they were, even Nancy's friends.

Nancy wafted by and kicked over his drink, without even noticing. "Come on, Asmodus, why don't you join in the fun a bit?"

"Nancy, my love, why don't you get some new friends?"

She wafted away again without bothering to answer.

"She's right, you know." Gordon, of the dark voice and twinkle, came over to share the wall and bring Asmodus a breath of sanity. Asmodus was fond of Gordon, an old knitting-companion from the Great Art Gallery Squat days. Gordon had taste. His flat was full of a lifetime's devotion to the theatre: curly photographs of starlets with crinkly hair and little black lips, a willowy poster for "Rapturous Dawn", a signed cigarette from Cocteau. Asmodus was surprised to find Gordon involved in one of Nancy's video-dramas.

"What have you done with Pink?" Gordon asked.

"He's over there, rolling something special."

Asmodus waved vaguely in the direction of the window. "It's his world première as well, you know. He's hung his new painting up for show, but I don't think anyone's noticed it."

"Excuse me then, I must go and tell him how much I like it."

A burst of laughter carried down from the far end, where Dasha, dressed up as the Tartar Prince for the last time, was holding court to a circle of Nancy's cast-offs. In the corner Stéphane sat smoking, watching the performance with a clouded expression of tenderness and pride, more suitable to touching intimacies, Asmodus thought, than tawdry public festivities. Stéphane seemed very strange this evening. Distant. Asmodus eased himself up and went over to talk to her.

"Stéphane, my love, are you enjoying yourself? Or are you hating it all as much as me?"

She turned to him with a half-smile. "No, I'm not hating it. I've had a bad day, that's all. I keep thinking either I should join in more, or just disappear."

"You people that do proper jobs, you all seem to have a terrible time. Pink's just as bad. He came home looking like a dog that's done a mess on the carpet. I've no idea what the matter is, he won't say. Not like him at all."

"I don't think he knows. Or," Stéphane corrected herself, too quickly, "he's like me, not wanting to spoil the party."

"Have you been talking to him, then? I rather thought you were avoiding each other. No? Have you really done anything bad enough to spoil the party?" Asmodus put his head on one side. Stéphane's eyes had gone the colour of iron again: they wouldn't give up their secrets.

"Not tonight," she said. "Let's talk about it tomorrow."

"As you wish. So," he continued, "you seem to be under the impression that we're all gathered here to have a wonderful time, celebrating ourselves. Have you ever been to a world première before?"

She smiled and shook her head. "Tell me what's going to happen."

"Thespians are the same the world over, I suppose, even Nancy's. They all like to get together and give each other awards. Nancy's going to get the Luminous Bum award for being the greatest videodramatist of all time," Asmodus said despairingly. "Pink made it, specially for the occasion."

He pointed out the award, squatting next to a pile of beer-cans, decently shrouded, for the time being, with a cushion cover. "but I've been to some of Nancy's parties. After the great Xanadu, and the award, the lights will stay out and everyone will rush about doing nasty, lustful things."

"That's the bit you're looking forward to." Dasha turned away from her charmed circle and stooped down, offering Asmodus and Stéphane a hand each. Out of the corner of her eye she saw Nancy working round to the monitor. "Quick, get up. Find ourselves somewhere comfortable before it all happens."

Gordon turned out the hurricane lamps, leaving only a circle of candles round a high table where the monitor stood. "Quiet please, everybody."

There was a general rustling in the corners with some mean words about the sort of people who took all the best seats, and then the conversation dropped to a few stray whispers. Gordon held up his hand.

"Ladies and gentlemen," he began, affecting to ignore an audible sigh from Asmodus, "ladies and gentlemen, the moment you have all been waiting for." He smiled, gratified by the applause. "In a moment, Xanadu will be before you in all its splendour. But first, a word of introduction – no, not from me, Asmodus, so stop *doing* that – from Nancy herself! Nancy." He stretched out his arm and made a graceful exit into the shadows.

"Thank you, thank you . . ." Nancy bowed from left to right, while she tried to think of something to say. "Well, what you're going to see isn't, in the beginning, I conceived something quite different. But when you come to creating something, that's the wonderful thing about creative art, it turns out, you know –

differently. It's all a matter of inspirational direction."

Asmodus smiled to himself, knowing that it was also a matter of there not being enough cash to pay for Nancy's dream costumes and sets, or even the odd ton of dry ice. But Nancy, my love, money is only a substitute for imagination.

"That's all," Nancy said. "Let's watch it now. It's all right to talk. It's without Word."

Gordon blew out the candles.

Xanadu. The titles were fine. Just the one word, over a long view of someone stumping about on a pair of sandals tied to his knees.

"Hey, Nancy," Dasha was curious. "Why'd he have to be on his knees all the time?"

There was a chorus of shushing. Nancy turned round irritably. "He's supposed to be a dwarf, got it?"

"Sorry, ma'am."

There was no more talking out loud. Yawns and fidgets there were, plenty of those, except in the crowd scenes when the whole audience leaned forward with avid intensity. Pink crept into the corner nearest Asmodus and sat cleaning his nails surreptitiously, frowning a little with the effort of trying to understand why everyone was always so enthralled to see themselves on television. All those people sitting there, every eye communing with a vision of itself as centre of the universe.

After the orgy, a few sacrificial maidens danced themselves to death and the building of Xanadu began, while the Tartar Prince made an interminable descent down the fire-escape. Curled up between Dasha and Asmodus, Stéphane stared fixedly at the action, trying to hide any special delight when Dasha was on screen and, when there was no Dasha to look at, trying, almost guiltily, to work out what the piece was about. After the endless descent, and even longer interlude of entertainment from Sabrina and Scrubbers. Stéphane let her attention wander, first to the beaming Asmodus, and then to Dasha who was watching it all with a look of complete unconcern. Dasha grinned down at her, fleetingly, and gave a little shrug.

Back to the screen, where Sabrina's numbers had given way to some more action. The Prince, in an underexposed murk, creeping up on something. The crown shining, guarded by the massive back of the cut-out ogre. As the Prince put his hand on the crown, the dwarf poked the ogre and woke him up, but too late. The Prince snatched the crown and ran away with it.

"We had to do this bit about a hundred times," Dasha whispered. "The ogre kept falling over." Poor terrible, sad ogre.

After this episode, the Prince seemed to lose interest in Xanadu. He turned his back on it and played with his new crown, putting it on, taking it off, gazing at himself reflected in it; keeping would-be thieves at bay by swiping at them with an enormous fly-swatter. Meanwhile, barbarian thespians were busy ripping the tinfoil off the walls in great swathes, laughing and shrieking. The Prince walked up the fire-escape, the sacrificial maidens reappeared, and for a sinking moment Stéphane thought that the whole thing was going to start all over again.

But she was spared that. As the picture began to fade, Gordon busied himself lighting the candles, and when the applause died down Asmodus arose to take the centre of the floor.

"My people, kings, queens and princes. And fantasts." He bowed to Stéphane. "We are here on the occasion of the World Première of Xanadu, not only to marvel at this most wonderful videodrama, which we have just witnessed, but to honour its creator, Nancy."

Stamping and whistling. "She's a genius," Sabrina called out. More cheering. Asmodus lifted his hand. "As we have been able to judge from Miss Slink's performance. However, without more ado, I call upon Mr Philip Knight to present the Honourable Nancy Whitton with the highest award ever made to a videodramatist, the Luminous Bum award for outstanding contributions to the universe."

It was the signal for Nancy to climb up on the table, protesting with radiant humility that this was the greatest moment of her life. Shyly, Pink handed her his masterpiece, lovingly sculpted from papier-mâché and finished with the last of the Hallowe'en paint.

Gordon joined her in the limelight, holding a microphone. "Can you tell us what your feelings are at this historic moment?"

"I love you all," Nancy gushed.

"And what was your purpose in making Xanadu?"

"Cosmic perception –"

"I see, that's wonderful. Wonderful. And where do you go from here?"

"I think," Nancy said, "the next one is going to be a piece about myself." She hurried on before he could interrupt again. "Of course my cosmic pieces are the most important for the public to see now, but probably they'll end up more preferring the one about me."

"Thank you, ladies and gentlemen. The Honourable Nancy Whitton!"

With the presentation over, the night wore on much as Asmodus had predicted: the shifting patches of darkness, beyond the circle of candles, writhed with the shadows of roaming, groaning bodies.

Asmodus, Dasha and Stéphane shuffled their mattress over to the arched window-bay, and lay down side by side to look up at the stars. The frost had begun to trace patterns outside the window-panes and there was a ring round the moon; no clouds and no dust to reflect the City's sodium-lights that often turned the sky a dull, sore colour. Tonight the sky was an endless black lake filled with stars, clustered hundreds, thousands of them appearing to shine wherever Stéphane fixed her eyes, and fading when she looked away.

The tide was going out, and the night-breeze carried the sound of the river far off, past the cold edges of the mud-banks and down to the marshes where the sea began. Listening to it, Stéphane felt a pang of restlessness and knew that the others felt the same: Dasha, lying with one arm round her on the inside, and the other arm round Asmodus who had turned his face away. They fell asleep like that, dreaming of following the river to places where they had never been. Even when the sun rose they hardly moved, only shifted a little closer to each other, wanting to stay asleep for ever.

And in the morning, Adam and Martin came.

*

Even a man gifted with more imagination than Adam would have been appalled by the sight: a debris of coughing, twitching lunatics strewn around the floor and piled into heaps at the edges. White faces among the discarded rags. Haggard, painted eyes, smeared yawning mouths. A strange smell was clouding the air.

He was so stunned that he didn't notice Stéphane at first, but when she opened her eyes he was staring straight at her, with a look of pure horror. It had never occurred to him. Not that. Stéphane herself at the wharf, sleeping with all those . . . on that mattress with two what? Were they men or women? The one with the beard was wearing earrings three inches long.

Adam closed his eyes and rocked back on his heels, wishing he was safely back in his office. At least he shouldn't have dragged Martin along with him. This could be a total disaster. He sucked in his breath, thrusting his hands deep into his pockets and contemplating the floor, his expression a mixture of panic and disgust. If you can keep calm when all round you are losing their heads, it means you're holding the axe. So. He looked up, calmly. He was still the one holding the axe, and it was up to him now. Everyone was waiting for him to begin.

He cleared his throat and indicated Mr Geering, the gentleman who owned the wharf, and to whom he, Mr Drake, was now responsible for the wharf's future. Future demolition, in fact. Adam allowed himself a thin smile as he repeated the word, demolition. It had come to his attention that there were people living illegally in the wharf. And living illegally in other people's wharves was an extremely grave offence. He looked around, gravely. There was no response. Most of the offenders seemed to have gone back to sleep. He started shouting at them. "I want you all out of here, gone, by mid-day tomorrow! I'm warning you, anyone found here after that will have to face the most serious consequences. Understand me." He held up his palm and smashed his fist into it. "You are to be gone tomorrow by *noon*."

Asmodus blinked. The young master was enjoying his own performance so much, petulantly playing himself in with badly-timed dramatics. Proper thespian material. Any minute now, Nancy would jump up and hail him as a genius. Poke her camera in his face. But Nancy was only staring at Adam, dazedly, with her mouth open.

Adam had begun strutting up and down, addressing the room at large with a few well-chewed opinions about the sanctity of private propery in general and the evils of trespass in particular. But Asmodus had stopped listening and switched his attention to the older man, the one standing still by the door, saying nothing. If he really was the wharf's owner, it was odd that he appeared to be taking even less interest in the proceedings than Asmodus. The man's eyes had swept round the room once, when he came in, flicking away from Stéphane as though stung, and then moving back, reluctantly, to stare at her and Dasha for a few seconds. He was gazing into open space now, trance-like, his face sunken and frozen, deep lines like scars stretching down his cheeks.

Asmodus frowned, sensing vaguely that he ought to remember where he had seen the man before. On the river? No, outside, in the courtyard. That was it. The stringy grey man who had made Stéphane smile, and then kissed her. Seen close to he was more impressive, taller than he had looked in the courtyard. A strong face, fine hair, and a silk suit. But grey, all grey. Like a statue that only came to life for a second, just before he followed Adam out of the door. He grasped at Pink's sketch of Dasha stuck on the wall and then, in a single gesture of cold hatred, tore it down.

*

Someone was knocking on the door of Stéphane's flat. She roused herself, half-heartedly, and peered out of the window, knowing what she was going to see down there. Martin's car. No, she couldn't face it. She wanted to hide under the table.

The knocking came again, more urgently. And a voice: "Please miss? Are you in? It's Evans."

She let her jaw relax in a grudging smile. So Martin had sent his chauffeur. She should have been annoyed at the intrusion, but she wasn't. She liked Evans. He was sane.

She opened the door.

"There you are, miss." He seemed relieved. "I've been looking all over for you. Mr Geering says it's very important to find you. And to give you this."

"Thank you." She took the letter, pausing to say, "I'm sorry you had so much trouble finding me." She had fled from the wharf hours ago, not long after Martin himself.

Evans stepped to one side, shaking his head. "No trouble. Mr Geering says to wait for a reply," he added respectfully.

"I see. Will you come in for a few minutes? Do sit down."

He sat upright on the sofa, his hands on his knees, while she scrawled a reply on the bottom of Martin's letter and stuffed it into a new envelope.

"Evans?" she licked the flap and stuck it down, thoughtfully.

"Yes, miss?"

"No, nothing." She handed him the letter. She'd wanted to thank him for running Martin's errands, for finding her, keeping her company for a few minutes, and reminding her that there was another world outside the wharf. One peopled with quiet, kind Evanses. She wanted to hug him.

That was so stupid, she thought, after he'd gone. For all she knew, Evans got drunk every Friday night and beat up his wife. The world was cruel, after all. Even apples were supposed to scream when you peeled them. Stéphane wondered whether she might be going mad, retreating from one fantasy into the next. A world full of Evans-fantasies? And after that? There is no world.

She fixed herself another drink and sat down to wait for Martin. He wouldn't be long. His letter had been a request to see her; her reply, a message to the effect that she would be in her flat till mid-afternoon. If he wanted to see her, she owed him that. But it wasn't going to be a pleasant visit. No doubt it would be very unpleasant indeed.

She flinched, remembering the morning's horrors. The way Martin looked at her, what he did to Dasha's portrait. Her own confessions to Asmodus, and Pink and Nancy. And Dasha. The hurt looks on their faces. The desperate need to run away by herself, somewhere quiet where she could think. She'd done a great deal of thinking in the hours since, starting with a letter to Harkness, enclosing her resignation.

She'd made up her mind what she was going to do. Her step-father had a place in the Tyrol; she'd go there, stay there completely on her own. Try honestly to make sense of what she wanted. Somewhere in the back of her head a thought lurked: four-year-old child, it can't be as simple as that. But she refused to let the thought out. She was tired, tired, tired. It would be that simple, once she had cut herself away from all that mess of feelings fouling up her mind. And Dasha? The lurking thought put out a new tentacle. Unbearable, to cut herself away from Dasha too. But right, necessary. No more leeching on other people's lives. No more Martin, no more Dasha, no more anybody. Good.

Brave new resolution. It might have been that, making her

light-headed, or it might have been the drink. In any case, she was ready for Martin when he came.

He was determined to be civilised. She must forgive him if he'd behaved badly at the wharf; he was only upset to see her, his Stéphane, in all that filth. But all the same, he wanted an explanation for it.

She made up something about being attracted by the carefree artistic life of the squatters: the sort of life she might have led herself, once. And so on. He moved over to sit beside her, nodding like a clockwork mandarin, trying to keep up with her train of thought, then letting it go while he pursued his own.

"It doesn't matter about the squatters," he said. "I know you had your reasons. They're just pathetic little people, failures. Do you want me to give them somewhere else to live?"

"Martin." She was astonished at him. He was still trying to be generous, after everything she'd done. "Can you find them a place?"

"I already have." There was a flat empty in one of his blocks beside a flyover: quite a lot of empty flats, in fact. "And with them out of the way, there's no problem is there?"

She looked lost.

"About you carrying on with the wharf project, I mean," he explained, patiently.

"But Adam said . . ."

"Adam got it wrong. If you weren't here, he'd have it. But it's still you I want."

She walked over to her table, sadly, and showed him the letter she'd written to Harkness.

"Tear it up," Martin ordered.

"No."

"You can't just give up. Everything you've worked for." He was telling her for her own good. "You'll regret it. Look, you're upset, I know. At least give yourself time to think it over."

"I've done enough thinking about it."

He gaped at her. It was impossible. She couldn't be walking out on her job. Going away. That meant leaving him as well, didn't it?

"Stéphane, you do still love me, don't you?"

She shook her head.

He accused her then, in a very quiet voice, of being a lesbian.

No, she didn't accept that.

He wasn't surprised. It was an ugly word. Anybody would be ashamed to be called that.

"I'm not ashamed of it, Martin. It's not an ugly word, it's just irrelevant."

"Don't be childish, it is relevant." The anger seeping back. "I'm talking about that woman at the wharf."

"Yes, I love that woman at the wharf. But that's a whole different point of view from yours. I'm not going to ring it round with one word, so that you can just write it off."

"It can't be you, behaving like this. You've been drinking."

"Yes."

He sidled away from her, overcome with regret at realising for the first time: she wasn't so different from the others, after all. Drinking made her ugly, the way it made all women ugly. Some things you had to write off, when you couldn't make allowances for them any more.

Outside in the street, he didn't stop to look up at her window. He knew she wouldn't be watching him go.

She was busy getting ready to go back to the wharf.

*

"This one's all right; It's warm. You'll need this."

Nancy held up a green woolly thing: with an enormous floppy collar. It was hideous.

Asmodus flapped his hand, tiredly. "That's what the man in the market told me when I found it. Oh, no, even I can't wear that. Essentials, my love, essentials. Trio isn't a luxury cruiser, you know. There's hardly room enough inside for me and Pink, never mind a vast wardrobe of amazing technicolour nightmares."

Nancy put the woolly thing aside, with regret. It had seemed like a good idea, helping Asmodus and Pink to pack. She knew what they were like; they wouldn't have any idea about what they needed to take away with them. But they weren't even trying to help her. All Pink worried about was taking Gabriel's Breastplate, and as for Asmodus, he didn't seem to want anything.

"All this stuff's only what we found in skips anyway," he said. "It can just as easily be thrown out again. Let someone else have fun with it. Skip to skip, dustbin to dustbin."

Nancy admitted defeat and sat down to stare at them both. Graciously, Asmodus lifted up his profile. "But we mustn't be morbid, must we? What are you going to do now, Nancy? Cheer us all up with tales of wondrous new videodramas."

Nancy shook her head. "I've got to go back home. My mother rang me up last week, I wasn't going to tell you. She's getting married again. She wants to show me off in a party frock at the reception, and prove to all her friends that I haven't turned into a vampire."

"I thought she didn't know where you lived?"

"She found out. When I said I didn't want to go, she got really nasty." Nancy hunched down against the wall, looking depressed. "She said I was just a constant worry to her, I made her ill worrying about what I was doing. So I told her not to, it's all right here, all the interesting people, all that. And then she said she didn't care if it was the most interesting place in the world, she said, it sounded as though nobody ever washed. You'd think she'd be proud of having her daughter do something different, wouldn't you? She isn't. She'd be much prouder if I married someone rich and gave her lovely little grandchildren."

"They only want what they think's going to make you happy."

"It didn't make *them* very happy, whose side are you on? Anyway, she kept on about not liking the sound of my friends, so in the end I told her I couldn't stand her friends either." Nancy paused, recollecting the searing moment in tranquility. "When I said that, she went all quiet. I said 'Mother, are you there?' And she said, 'Very well, Nancy, we will leave the subject of your friends. I have something else I wish to ask you. I was looking for my wedding-dress. Where is it?'"

Asmodus cackled, enquiringly.

"Well, I was engaged once," Nancy mumbled, looking ashamed. "I was engaged to . . . never mind who. And Mother gave me her old wedding-dress, as though it was an heirloom, or something, in a sort of *ceremony*, really creepy. Then I wasn't engaged any more, so her old dress wasn't any use to me, I just got rid of it when I came down here. I gave it to this theatre crowd I used to know."

Asmodus guffawed. It was the first time he'd laughed, properly laughed, all day. Nancy looked offended. "It wasn't funny. I don't know what she wanted it for, how was I to know? In the end I had to tell her I'd given it away. She hit the roof."

Asmodus tried to look sympathetic and helpful. "Couldn't you get it back for her?"

"It wouldn't be any good. They tore bits off it and flicked it all over with brown paint. They were very into conceptual art . . . ."

She broke off and looked across at Pink, who was hugging his knees and rocking himself on the floor. His cheeks were wet.

"Angel, don't cry."

Asmodus put his arms round Pink and stroked his hair.

"Please don't cry," echoed Nancy. He reminded her of something she'd seen at one of her mother's jumble-sales: a worn-out teddy bear sitting in the middle of a junk-stall. She bit her lip, not wanting to listen to the things he was blurting out. He didn't want to leave the wharf, people didn't understand, they thought old things were ugly, destroyed them without knowing, that sometimes things grew old with too much loving.

Nancy forgot about her mother and began to hate Stéphane instead, for causing all this. It was a terrible thing to have done to Asmodus and Pink. Nancy told them so, adding a few spiteful ideas of her own about what they ought to do with Stéphane. Most of the ideas involved a complete destruction of the drainage pipes. It was all right for Stéphane, wasn't it, she had money and everything. It was all right for her to go around having fun at the wharf and then give the whole game away, and sit watching everyone else drown themselves in the mess she'd made.

"No no, no no," Asmodus crooned, still rocking. "Charity, my love, you've no idea, have you? It's no use blaming her, it's not her fault. Don't be silly, none of us are drowning, we're just moving on to new things, that's all, and it's probably time, don't you think? Her too. She's no different from us now – Agh!" He felt something pricking around the small of his back and reached behind himself, cautiously, with one hand.

"Aha! Gotcha, you little menace." His hand returned to view, firmly clutching a squashed-looking Nero. "A pound and half of nasty little ginger tomcat. Eh?" He turned the kitten over on its back and began to tickle its stomach. It wrapped its front paws round his hand, grimly, and battered away at his wrist with its back legs. "That's enough of that now." Asmodus pulled a piece of wool from somewhere about his person and tied a cigarette-paper to the end of it, drawing it along the floor so that Nero ran after it, waggling and patting and pouncing.

"Little Pink, are you laughing?" With his free arm, Asmodus gave Pink a squeeze and passed the end of the wool over to him. "Come on, Nancy, help me make something to drink."

"What about the cats?" she asked him, taking turns at warming hands over the kettle. "You're not just going to leave them here, are you?"

"Why not? Best place for them. You don't want them, I take it."

"No, but all the same . . . Messalina's huge again. Somebody ought to make sure she's all right."

"Take her then, if you want to find kittens in the bottom of your bed every morning. Or worse," Asmodus added darkly. "That cat is a psychopath."

All right, perhaps Messalina wasn't such a deserving case after all. But what about the kittens? "What's going to happen to them? They're so sweet."

Asmodus sighed impatiently. "My love, Nero and Caligula are not sweet. *None* of them are sweet little pussies. They're wharf-cats! Half-wild! That's their life, the rats and the birds and the wide-open spaces. They're not people! They don't want to live in a flatlet, and go to sleep on top of the television and eat Catto three times a day. They'd rather –"

"– Just because you don't –"

"– be made into fur coats. What? No, quite right. I don't want to either." Asmodus corrected himself. "We don't want to. Not me or Pink."

"I think this idea of you just sailing off in the boat is crazy," she told him flatly. "Crazy. Where do you think you're going?"

Asmodus said nothing.

"The owners," she persisted. "They should find you somewhere. Can't you make them? Stay here till they do? they'll have to."

"Oh, you still don't understand, do you?" His voice had a faint note of despair in it. "Yes, they would. I can't go on explaining it again, I've been through all this once before this evening, with Stéphane. *She'll* find us a place. The *owners* will. The Social Security, Humpty Dumpty and all the King's men. They'll all find us a place and it's very kind of them. Do we want their places, that's the thing. Frankly, my love, no. We can't be doing with rent books and gas meters and things like that, all cooped up. How can we be ourselves," ending his speech with drama, his hand on his heart, "how can we be ourselves in a place somebody else has decided we ought to live in?"

He turned round and poured out the kettle, thoughtfully, balancing a tray while he stood and looked out into the darkness. "Well, my love, the night begins. Do share it with us. Then you can be here in the morning, to participate in the grand going-away ceremony."

"No, I don't think so." She kissed his beard, with infinite fondness. "No, please, I couldn't stand watching you go. I can't bear endings." She tried to smile. "That's why my pieces never have endings."

Or beginnings, or middles, Asmodus thought, smiling back at her to show he understood.

"I couldn't bear it," she said again. "What I want to do is this, just say good-bye and walk out, just go away, like I've always done before, and think that I can come back, anytime, and find you still here."

*

"Why didn't you tell me this was going to happen?" Dasha's voice was rough. "Just why didn't you tell me? And don't say I never asked."

She had finished throwing her clothes in a suitcase. It hadn't taken long. She had left most of the morning for packing up her photographs and slides: things that were worth taking care over. Moodily, Stéphane sat watching. Dasha glaring through the occasional negative; the fierce meticulous movements of Dasha's fingers slotting little coloured squares into boxes. Why so much anger all of a sudden, left till the last moment?

"I was afraid you wouldn't want to see me any more," Stéphane said simply, "if I told you what I was really doing here."

"Sweetheart, I can make up my own mind about whether I want to see you. I don't need you to work it out for me."

"Well, I wasn't going to risk it, that's all." Stéphane didn't feel like apologising; she'd done enough of that last night. If only she had the will-power to get up and leave. If only.

"You can't have trusted me very much," Dasha pointed out, "if you couldn't even risk that."

"Oh, I don't know. Don't go on at me. I don't know what I thought."

"You know now? You still want to go away and be the old man on the mountain?"

Stéphane sighed. "Yes, yes, yes."

"You're wrong."

"Why didn't you say so last night then?" Stéphane flared up. "I thought you understood? Didn't you?"

"I listened to you. Listening to you is enough to make a saint weep, all that stuff about wanting to be by yourself. But it's wrong, and I'd have told you that last night, if I thought you meant it."

"When I say something, I usually do mean it."

"Ain't that the truth. Don't we all mean what we say, when we're saying it. But we might not mean it the next morning."

Dasha went back to her pictures. "What are you still here for, then? A touching farewell? Ah. You'll know when I took this one. In your flat when we spent all afternoon in bed, remember? The day it rained."

She held the photograph against the wall and thrust a pin through it. "Isn't it beautiful? You can have it. Everyone needs happy memories when they're alone, and they start asking themselves –"

"Why make it so hard?"

"Pity it's only black and white. Maybe you can get it tinted. What colour would you like it to be? Rose? Gold and silver? Marble?"

Dasha took out a grey-blue blue filter and held it up to the light, narrowing her eyes to stare through it at their bodies fixed with a pin. Lips bruised, salt-tasting, aching hands searching, the sting of fingernails, and rake of a shoulderblade. I love you, oh, I love you.

Slowly, Dasha put down the filter and leaned back against the table.

"Will you look at me now?"

Stéphane winced and lifted up her head.

"I'll tell you this much, I know," Dasha said. "My life's still going to make sense, with you or without you." She scratched her lip. "Only being with you makes a different kind of sense, all by itself. I can't help that."

She pushed herself away from the table and began to walk up and down the room, taking snapshots in dumb-show. "You still here? Who's going to leave first, you or me? You don't have to listen to me. I'm not sure I want to listen to me any more either."

"No, go on. I'm listening to you." Stéphane's voice was eager, as though she wanted a reason for staying. "Go on. I'm listening."

"All right then." Dasha dropped her arms and stood still, looking somewhere over the top of Stéphane's head, talking to the wall. "You want to run away and sit on top of an alp, all by yourself. Sure you can do that. You can contemplate your own everlasting self till the sky falls down. But when you've done it, all you end up with is you. Still only you. That going to be enough? Because if that's all you know, it'll have to be." She broke off, tiredly, thinking of Asmodus, and made a last effort to bring her feelings home. "You know what matters to me most, every time I take a picture? The difference between what a thing is, and how it looks. Take you. You can know yourself – more or less – by what you think and feel, how you are. But you only know other people by how they look. How do you know what you look like to them?"

Stéphane sat back, crossed her legs, and put on a wooden expression. "Does it matter?"

"Why, no. Just shut your eyes and they'll all disappear. You do that, you can imagine yourself to be anything you want. You can be the sun and the moon and the Second Coming all rolled into one, and you don't even have to sit on top of an alp, to be that. All you do is blot out anyone who might just hint they don't see you the way you see yourself."

"Stop it." Stéphane broke in, edgy and miserable. "Just stop it. Don't go on like that. I don't want to be the sun or the moon or anything else, except me. Understand? I want to make sense of me." She stabbed herself with her fingers. "Me, me, me. All right?"

"You want to make sense of you, don't you know anything? That's what love's *for*." Dasha whipped around twice on the spot, cracking her knuckles. But when she spoke again her voice was even. "Only someone who loves you can show you to yourself. Because only someone who loves you really cares who you are. Right, let's all go home now."

She turned away to bend over a carton, placing the boxes in it one by one and then sealing it with the huge roll of brown tape. The room blurred in front of Stéphane, seeming to grow wider, hollow and cold, filling itself with the sickening tearing screech of tape being ripped off and stuck down.

The noise stopped.

"Oh," Dasha groaned, "you're not crying again, are you? Did I do that? Did I make you cry? Me and my stupid mouth." She left her boxes and crouched down in front of Stéphane, holding out her hands. "Here I am. You want to throw something at me? I never saw anyone cry as much as you."

"Don't you ever cry?"

"Only when everyone else is asleep."

"When I said all those things to you last night?"

"Ah, didn't you fall asleep afterwards?"

"So I did." Stéphane bent her head and put Dasha's hands round her neck. "Never let me do that again."

"I never will, Fantast; I never will."

Stéphane breathed in, a long fragrant inspiration of heart-easing belief. Being with you makes a different kind of sense. Even if I don't know why, not yet. How should I know what it's about?

Thinking of that, she laughed.

"Mm?"

"Something Nancy said."

"May she be forgiven." Dasha smiled out at the river, and stood up. The morning was almost gone. Going-home time. She thought of Paris as she had seen it last, under the wing of an aeroplane.

"Wonderful, sweet Fantast. You." Dasha picked up her carton of slides, and presented it. "This one's yours."

In the car, Stéphane unfolded the blanket on the back seat and wrapped the carton up in it, fussing over it at length, tucking in the corners, making very sure it was well padded.

"You still fiddling over that?" Dasha locked up the boot and walked round to give the blanket a poke. "C'mon, it's only a box of pictures."

"Get off, let me wrap it up how I like. So's to keep it safe. What next?"

"The grand going-away ceremony." Dasha checked her watch and then stood looking up at the west wall, smiling a little to herself and thinking how beautiful the mornings could be here, when the early winter sun glanced across the river. Somehow it never seemed to rain when Asmodus and Pink held a ceremony. "Let's go wait for them by the jetty. They should be down soon."

*

"Will they be long now?" Stéphane linked hands with Dasha and walked over to the window; the same window where Asmodus had poked his head out, the first day she saw him. "What are they waiting for?"

"They're giving us time alone together." Dasha raised her eyebrows in mock bafflement at such a quixotic idea. "To make sure we're going to be all right, after they've left us all by ourselves. They'll be spying on us from some hidey-hole right now, so let's have a kiss for their benefit."

"Are you all right, really?" she asked more seriously, when the benefit performance was over. She turned to lean out of the window, resting her arms on the sill. Asmodus had given her a parting gift, a couple of thin steel chains that she wore round her wrist; they clashed faintly and glinted in the river-light, throwing speckled patterns against the stonework.

Stéphane watched the patterns for a while, and then let her eyes rest on the movement of the water outside. She'd only watched the river from this window once before. The tide was on the wane then, flowing from behind her, dark with all the rubbish it had picked up on its way. Now, it was flowing towards her. Not going out with the drifts of what might have been, but sweeping in the promise of what might be, born out of the future.

"Yes," Stéphane said, "I'm all right."

"Dasha! Stéphane! Are you still waiting for us, down there?"

Asmodus bustled in. "Ah, good. It's time, my loves. You may pipe us down the ladder, if you wish. No, not if you wish. It's an Imperial Command." The Hallowe'en plastic flute and toy drum were presented. "Since the ghost didn't come to dance when we played them, he can just sit and listen while we go. Serve him right."

First Asmodus, then Pink, squeezed and grunted through the window, scrabbling on the sill, fishing for the rope ladder with their feet, while Dasha and Stéphane made a din, cheerfully, to cover up any crotchety moments that might happen to spoil the grand descent.

Asmodus made his way gingerly up to the bows and settled down, as comfortably as he could, given that he had to sacrifice half the space to Gabriel's Breastplate. He was clutching a cushion and trying to push it underneath himself without capsising the boat. He abandoned the attempt at last, tossed the cushion over the side, and looked up. Serenely.

"Well, my loves, here we are about to set off on our great journey. Rowing up and down the world. Isn't it a pity we can't find room for you sinners, in our magic boat? Would you come with us, if you could? Or do you want to be left beind?"

"Where are you going?" Stéphane asked.

"We don't know," Pink replied simply. Asmodus silenced him with a look. "Is there anything else you want to ask, my loves?"

"We never saw the ghost, did we?" said Dasha.

"No, well, that's how ghosts are." Asmodus pointed his nose into the wind, seeming to blink away the sting of the icy, dry air. "I don't suppose we'll be seeing each other again, will we?"

Dasha protested. "Why not? Who knows?"

"I know." Asmodus held up his hand in a gracious gesture of farewell. "Angel, you're supposed to push the boat out now. We can't just sit here till my hand turns to wood. Come along, do."

Pink stood up, reluctantly, bracing his legs against the wobble of the boat, and held his oar out for a moment towards the two women. Then he set it against the wall and heaved.

The boat eddied out into the creek while Pink took his time, sitting down again and arranging his oars about him. When everything was right he began to pull away towards the river, slowly at first, then picking up more speed as the current took them.

"Let's watch them from the Singing Gallery." Dasha put her hand on Stéphane's arm and drew her away.

Running up made them too breathless to say anything else to each other. They grabbed hold of the furthest casement frame and tugged at it, urgently, until it gave with a harsh grinding noise, to let them lean out. Pink and Asmodus were still in sight, making their stately progress down the river flowing thirty feet below. The Singing Gallery was more silent than Stéphane had ever known it, not even a whisper to break the hush, straining to catch the fragments that floated back on the wind.

". . . Yea, though we pass through the valley of the dolls . . .".

"Don't buzz me, Asmodus . . . I got to row this thing straight."

". . . O bring me a boat that will carry us twain, and we shall row . . . my love and I . . . ."

The boat slid out of sight round a bend, and the Gallery was still again.

Stéphane and Dasha stayed side by side for a long while, looking out over the water, listening to all the familiar wharf-sounds that began to creep back again and soften the emptiness. The river sucking at the walls, loose chains grating against the stonework. And when they drew their heads in at last and closed the window, they noticed a small of cloves lingering.

They walked away, back out of the Gallery, past the Torture Chamber and the Vault of Loneliness, down the grand staircase, and out into the courtyard.

Dasha tapped at her watch. "Fantast, it's time to go." It was four minutes to twelve. By noon, the man said. It was his turn now.

They smiled at each other and took hold of the tall iron gates, one on each side. Then they walked out together into Quadrant Street, closing up the wharf behind them.

Brilliance Books is a gay and lesbian imprint and we welcome manuscripts on all subjects by gay and lesbian writers.

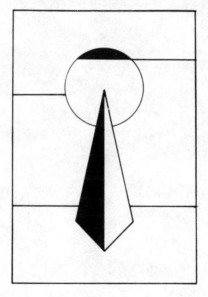